Cameron R Spence is a newly published author from a tiny place that no one has ever heard of (unless you've read the back of a Carlsberg can), Northampton. He is known for his frank and unique outlook on the rebellious experiences of the young adults in his family and friends (of which there aren't many).

His dark sense of humour can polarise some, but that's neither here nor there.

Having done nothing with his life, Cameron Spence delved into the world of writing. When he isn't writing or self-deprecating, he is probably with his dog or painting.

*Perspective* is his debut novel.

For you.

Cameron R Spence

# PERSPECTIVE

AUSTIN MACAULEY PUBLISHERS™

LONDON • CAMBRIDGE • NEW YORK • SHARJAH

A CIP catalogue record for this title is available from the British Library.

ISBN 9781528994576 (Paperback)
ISBN 9781528994583 (Hardback)
ISBN 9781528994590 (ePub e-book)

www.austinmacauley.com

First Published (2020)
Austin Macauley Publishers Ltd
25 Canada Square
Canary Wharf
London
E14 5LQ

# Prologue

Everything has a beginning, a middle and an end; something everyone has been conditioned to accept from day one. What about the parts in between, the transition? The change is something nobody ever really gets used to. I mean, how do we truly know when one thing has ended and it's time for another to begin? For example, we are born and we live the first few years as an infant, then we move on to childhood, then young adulthood and so on, but where is the line? Where's the divide? Who decided that we when we live the first five years of our lives that we're ready to start learning about the world around us? Who decided that after the first 13 that our bodies would become ready to have sex? Who decides when we're ready to 'grow up'? I know, it's refreshing to hear adolescent angst along the lines of an identity crisis or whatever but that's not what this is.

Christopher Isherwood once said:

*I am a camera with its shutter open, quite passive, recording, not thinking.*

It sums up all I am and all I ever will be, for that is exactly what I am, a camera that does not think but still takes it all in and reacts. This is the reaction. That is all.

I know exactly who I am.; I'm just not sure whether I like it.

\*\*\*

Wake up. That's all I had to do. Wake up; drag myself out of bed to greet the New Year. As my tired limbs slowly shifted from beneath my duvet, my whole body felt numb and lifeless. January never was my favourite time of year. This year, however, in an extremely 'Bridget Jones' fashion, would be different from the others. For starters, I was not going to allow myself to mope for another three hundred and sixty-five days about how ridiculously pathetic I am. Next on the agenda was to attempt to silence the enormous alcoholic monkey on my back, or at least quiet him down a bit. Finally, do something important with my year. Anything of significance would do, if for no other reason, to break the incredibly boring cycle that has been the last eighteen years of my mundane life.

Waking up is the hardest part of the day, you never feel like yourself in those first few seconds. Forcing ourselves from a completely silent world of our own and moving us forward into the big wide world ready to face the day, where's the sense in that? From the moment we open our eyes in the morning choice upon choice is thrown our way, like what to dig up from the pile of clothes on the floor to wear today, or what to eat for breakfast, whether or not I'll be in a good mood today and whether or not to leave the house and do something productive. More conditions and more routines, it's not that I particularly mind, it just is.

My bare feet met with the linoleum of my bedroom floor, pretentiously made to look like 'real wood', carefully selected by my mother to match the awkwardly modern design of the rest of my room. In keeping with the modern design, I had to move no further than ten inches before reaching a sink strategically placed in front of my shower. It's important to note at this point, by no means do I mean I had an En suite bathroom. I literally had a small ceramic sink and a shower inches away from my bed. I couldn't quite decide whether or not that's a good thing. On one hand I'm no more than ten inches away from the sink, but on the other I'm no more than ten inches away from the sink. Either way, as the cold floor tickled my feet and I managed to stagger towards the sink, I caught sight of my reflection

What exactly did I see? A boy, about five feet and nine inches tall, pale skin and dark hair that's kept purposefully longer on top than at the sides; his name is James, James Harlot. I wouldn't say the face I saw was particularly unattractive but at the same time I wasn't about to wink charmingly before flexing my non-existent muscles and moving swiftly on. An average sized male with an average face for an extremely average existence. God, even as I write I can envision these printed words processed through a cheap filter and slapped on Tumblr. Two eyes, blue, staring directly back at me. They filtered through the idea that I would have to become an active member of society; unless of course I decide to crawl back into bed and never resurface. I could see the headlines already:

*Mildly Attractive Teenage Skeleton Found Under Duvet*
*Caressing Empty Ice Cream Boxes*

What was that resolution? No more moping, "Active member of society it is!" I said out loud to myself.

Coffee is the lord's saving grace to any cold and miserable morning. I am a firm believer that anyone who says they're a morning person without any extra stimulant is a liar. As I took a sip of the bittersweet morning glory, I was ready to become me. Now I could face whatever lay ahead for the day, with unprecedented optimism of course. The usual combination of skinny jeans and awkwardly oversized knitted jumper would be the pull-out choice for today; as with most days if I'm honest, before taking another look in the mirror.

What exactly did I see? Me, about five feet and nine inches tall, pale skin and dark hair that's kept purposefully longer on top than at the sides; my name is James Harlot. An average sized male with an average face for an extremely average existence.

In winter, the streets always made me feel like I was part of a profound, one-off BBC TV drama, the kind with a lot of unexplainable slow-motion shots of me walking down along the pavement, having just had a life-changing epiphany. The story of a young boy that learns that it's ok to be different, that 'he's not alone in this world' and whatever other cliché the writers could think to throw in. Ray LaMontagne or Damien Rice would feature on the soundtrack. Not that I have a problem with any of the above, I am just far from profound and the real nature of me leaving the house was that I had made plans with a friend to get very stoned, what's profound about quite literally smoking my life away out of boredom? Nothing. A few minutes of walking with my headphones bleeding unbearably loud music and I was there. I've always found it handy to live so close to such a good friend, my best friend in fact.

The fresh, crisp air chilled the inside of my nose as I edged towards the front door. No car in the front drive, this meant her mother was out of the house—perfect! I knocked. I could immediately hear the muffled sound of footsteps frantically searching for the keys. Something about leaving the door locked when you're home has never appealed to me. It just means morons like me wait on the doorstep three times longer than needed. The door clicked as the lock turned and the door flew open. There she was, tall and slim with a mess of dyed red hair loosely hanging over her shoulders.

"You're late!" she said to me as I stepped through the door and into the hallway.

I smiled and gave her a friendly hug, sarcastically retorting, "Sorry Anna, I was having a deep existential crisis and couldn't decide whether I wanted to get out of bed this morning."

"Shut the fuck up and start rolling," she joked. She handed me a small zip lock bag and a pouch of tobacco. I laughed back and made my way into her kitchen grabbing an old Yale key that sat by the microwave. The kitchen door clicked open and I entered the back garden, key in one hand and tobacco in the other. Immediately, the cold air hit me as I meandered to the left, leaving the door open behind me, my converse slipping slightly on the icy decking. There it stood. A decaying brick shed hiding in the corner of her garden. The outer plaster was peeled and flaking away exposing the orange mossy bricks beneath, surrounded by gravel and weeds. It was a hideout for us. Our refuge. I have no doubt that my GCSE English teacher would say that the shed was some symbol for the decomposition of our innocence and its decaying settings was just "juxtaposing our perfectly happy situation" etc. But no, it was, and simply, is a place to do whatever we wanted and not get questioned about any of it. I let myself in. The smell of damp was expected and a cloud of dust flew into the air as I flung myself onto the faded orange sofa that idly sat in the corner of the tiny, worn out shed. A few minutes passed and I had done what Anna had asked and she had joined me in the shed with a lit candle in hand. Apparently, the economy was in too much of a bad state for us to be able to afford lighters or whatever other witty remark she could come up with.

She sat on the floor as she inhaled the first drag of my poorly constructed joint. The earthy scent filled the air as she passed it forward. Anna slowly edged back and rested her head on the floor, gazing idly at the ceiling, following a trail of smoke. Minutes passed and we continued to pass joint after joint back and forth to each other. We sat in silence mostly until she caught sight of another trail of smoke.

"Smoke is so beautiful. I wish I was smoke, and then I'd be just as beautiful."

"Yeah, but then after a few seconds you'd be gone forever," I replied.

"At least in those few seconds I'd be the most beautiful thing ever. Better to feel beautiful for a few seconds than never at all."

That was singularly the most insightful thing I had ever heard. And it came from someone who was baked like Dr Oetker, what does that honestly say about everything? I mean we live in an age where people who haven't even completed puberty are taking class-A drugs and having orgies. Yet Anna and I sit on the floor of a dirty shed talking about being smoke.

"Anna, let's go somewhere and do something, please?" I said.

She sat up slightly, looked me dead in the eye, cleared her throat and said "Food first, productivity later."

I of course laughed and we made our way to the kitchen. I lifted myself on the kitchen counter, reaching for a box of cereal and helped myself. The first wave of light headed euphoria hit me as Anna joined in on the dry cereal feast.

"I'm going to move away from here one day," I said resentfully. Anna scoffed, and then scoffed some more as she loaded her mouth.

"As long as you take me with you."

That was a few years before. Give or take. As the warm bath water around me started to turn cold, I looked up with a glassy eyed blank expression. My bathroom ceiling became a white washed reverie as I came crashing back to reality. A siren sounded in the distance as I moved my eyes towards a green, square bottle that rest upon my bathroom tiles. My resolution didn't stick apparently. As the bitter taste of gin burned my throat I slipped back into the water and let it grow even colder. Another siren sounded.

As I placed the bottle back onto the floor, I lifted myself from the bathtub and joined it there on the cold bathroom tiles. Once again, I found myself looking into the mirror. Two eyes, blue but slightly bloodshot, pale skin, dark hair. It looked like a boy, a man some people might argue, but all I saw this time was smoke.

# Chapter 1
## *Track 1 – The Sundays,*
## *God Made Me*

Every morning is the same. A collection of measured time, from the moment the abusive and irritating alarm sounds, that seems to run out quicker with each passing day. What used to be a 6.30am start turns into a 7.45am rush for the train, what used to be 25 minutes for breakfast and a shower turns into a biscuit and a spray of the nearest available perfume. Quickly swallowing four painkillers and washing them down with whatever was available before leaving the apartment and entering street level; an active member of society. I was one of them now, I was just another commuter that has to push and force myself onto the train before I ended up an hour late for the job I didn't actually enjoy. This was of course amplified by the fact that I had a canary wharf wannabe's armpit in my face for the majority of the journey and apparently, he didn't have time for a shower either. I tried to hold a chesty cough in the back of my throat but it forced its way from my body and I could feel everyone's eyes on me; the taste of copper and stale alcohol hit my tongue and I, now more than ever, felt people's eyes on me.

Regardless of how invisible I am on the morning commute I can't help but feel an unwarranted pressure to carry myself with confidence. It's almost as if every other person in the world is looking at me and if I don't have every inch of confidence on my face then it's game over. Life is a game of retail. We are constantly selling ourselves, consciously or not. When you start telling the story of how your weekend went to a relative, when you put your makeup on in the morning, when you crawl out of bed at three in the afternoon and wander into the streets with no care in the world you are selling yourself to. You want people to believe the stories and invest their time in you and give you the satisfaction of being noticed. As we've all experienced, the sales pitch isn't necessarily the product you are getting. Weather you care to admit it or not, that's what's happening every moment of every day. We all do it and we are all guilty of doing it to other people.

I liked to play a game on the daily commute. I called it 'guess the sales pitch', whereby I took a look at the general public and saw what they were portraying versus what they are, for example:

1. Tall guy, dark hair, well dressed and carrying a brown leather suitcase. That usually translates as a confident businessman.
   - In actual fact he's a middle-aged prick with a long list of ex-lovers and probably has a fetish for dominatrix's
2. A blonde, muscular, ripped jeans wearing beard with his hand grabbing at every arse it sees
   - translates as closet homosexual
   - probably also has a fetish for dominatrix's

And well, you get the picture. I can't help but wonder how many people have done the same with me as I pushed my way through the mass of workers. How many people noticed me at all? The underground becomes such a beautiful place in the morning; it turns into a clockwork beehive. Every individual face blurs into one rushing mass, all as eager to jump on the train that will have another one arrive in less than a minute. This mass has no concept of time other than the fact that they'll be late if they don't squeeze themselves onto the train that's about to close its doors potentially losing an arm or every shred of dignity for that morning. So, with that in mind, the world seemed so much smaller.

In such a small world, it's surprisingly easy to get lost, and in a large crowd of people, it's surprisingly easy to feel alone and with all of these large crowds in such a small world, it's so very easy to find that something is missing. There's a large gap inside of every one of the worker bees in the clockwork hive. These gaps then form their own large spaces that need to be filled; everybody knows that. But what if these gaps can't be filled? What if these busy worker bees in the large crowds of the small worlds can't fill those large gaps? Do they wonder empty? Do they live with it? Of course, the two aren't mutually exclusive, it's perfectly possible to wander empty and live always having something missing. The real question is; how long can this go on? Suddenly it all makes sense, every irrational argument you've had with a lover or every time you've had more to drink than you should have or every time you've ran for that train that you know you can't make; it's all to fill the gap. To distract ourselves and to keep it at bay, just for a little while.

Then the distraction ended. I found myself anxiously making my way in through the front entrance of the shop, ready for work and ready to become an active member of society. My eyes scanned the floor for any sign of my manager; a feeble and repugnant man. The sort of man that you might avoid if you had any choice but somehow when you did interact with him you couldn't help but laugh and enjoy his company. A person who was a walking contradiction, this allowed me to work for him resentfully, but maintain a level of camaraderie that resembled friendship. An enjoyably loathsome experience; like listening to the latest Taylor Swift single in a nightclub. I stood there silent for some time removing my bag and adjusting to the idea that I would be stood in the same place for the next six hours.

"Morning!" the high pitched and overly joyful tone resonated through my ears as he appeared from beneath the counter.

I smiled. The masquerade begins. I stood vacant as he reeled off every task for the day ahead, pretending to take the slightest bit of interest in everything he had to say; I knew where this was ultimately going to end up. It was the same thing most days, besides today was a Thursday and that meant it was my turn to close late and that also meant that he would find any excuse to stay late with me.

On a side note, let me just say that anyone who claims working in retail is easily a liar. They are a liar and there is no other explanation. Sure, certain aspects of it are easy, processing sales and standing around all day is fairly easy but that isn't what working in retail is, that's what you as a customer are shown. Contrary to popular belief, the customer is not always right, in fact they are usually wrong and an asshole. If you have ever impatiently pushed in line, or gotten angry with a sales consultant for the price of something or not listened to them when told you can't return something because it doesn't fall within their policy, you too are an asshole. But hey, I'm not here to scald the innocent, I am fully aware that the majority of the general public have no idea that they are the problem when it comes to shopping so I'm going to give you some golden rules to live by; remember these people are providing you with a service, they are doing you a favour, act like it.

1. If you are in the middle of a phone call, DO NOT enter the shop, wait and allow everyone else to enjoy their day. All are very important, wait your turn or don't wait at all. It makes everyone involved very uncomfortable.
2. Saying 'Please' and 'Thank you' makes everyone's day better. NEVER demand something, avoid using words like 'let me have' or 'give me' – Frankly it's rude as shit and no one wants to help you.
3. If the stores doors are closed or the shutters are down a bit, and I can't stress this enough, do not try and shop. If you encounter this, ask yourself "can I get in and out in two minutes or less?" if the answer is no then leave and return the next morning. To be honest, the shop has probably been open nine hours prior stop leaving things until the last minute.

**4.** And lastly, if you ask a question, try your hardest not to get offended by the answer. Do not attempt to keep asking the question in hopes of getting a different answer, it doesn't work like that. Unless it falls under policy you can't return it, there's nothing we can do about the price unless you have a voucher and no if it doesn't scan it is not free, that joke was never funny GET OUT.

Back to the story; I dealt with those five rules every single day. Within the last hour I was counting down every single minute that was left. The reasons for me wanting to leave so urgently are still unclear, a part of me wanted to be in bed sleeping all day and another part of me just wanted to be at home endlessly watching Buffy, the Vampire Slayer. That's when the inevitable happened. The shops shutters dramatically closed on the hour, of course I had the key to do so which filled me with a sense of power no one had ever managed; it was as if I were able to command the people. I was called to the stockroom. The metallic shelves lined the walls filled with excess product. In the corner sat a white telephone and a few post-it notes. A part of me wanted to draw crude doodles on the post-its, detailing everything I knew to be true.

The metallic shelves shook as I was thrust upon them in a heated passion, my back felt bruised by the force. He fell to his knees and unzipped my trousers; this was it. It had happened before, but now it was a habit. There was a part of me that couldn't help myself, by all means I was not attracted to this man but something allowed me to enable his passions on me. I looked directly at the top of his head and groaned with feigning interest as the shelving units behind me shook once more. I looked to the ceiling and closed my eyes as my mind went blank. A few minutes passed. I could feel his mouth on me and his breath had never felt as enticing as this moment, I knew it was wrong. Then, as if it came from a different part of me that didn't exist yet, I could feel the energy surging through me. I could feel the exact reason as to why I let this happen. "I'm going to cum!" I murmured, as he nodded. It happened and he swallowed every part of me. Immediately after I had orgasmed, I felt an astonishing sense of grief, as though I had lost myself. I felt as though a part of me has been taken. This was of course to be met with a casual sense of normality. He stood up making eye contact with me as I bent over and quickly pulled my work trousers up to hide my nakedness. "I'm disgusting!" I mimed to myself, turning away, as an itch began to grow in my throat. The itch spread and overwhelmed my body as my feet began to twitch and I rapidly tapped my fingers at my side. We parted ways as I ended the day as I had begun, with a commute.

This time I became one of the rushing bees, swerving and dodging the hive, risking life and limb to catch the first possible train as I had so effortlessly mocked others for doing before. I couldn't shake the urge to reach the other side of my journey, to reach home and soothe the burning in my throat. The journey seemed more important this time. An hour passed as my train pulled to its final stop, allowing me to leave the hive and continue alone. My front door had never seemed more important than this moment as if everything behind the door could ease the guilt, I felt boiling up inside of me. My key couldn't work fast enough as my hands shook with anticipation. Then I stopped. I stood in the silence of my hallway, leaving the street behind and entering my own world. To my right was the kitchen and straight ahead lay a dark corridor leading to an empty living room. I turned right. Feeling for the light switch, I remained silent. I stopped and listened silence. I flicked the switch as the humble kitchen dimly began to illuminate. I stopped again thinking for a moment. The small square room left a lot to be desired with just the basic requirements and all-around vinyl countertops; a large plastic bin sat beneath the counter directly opposite me. Behind the bin was a small panel leading to gas pipes, presumably they had some significance to the well-being of my home; for me, they had a completely different significance all together. Slowly I knelt on the floor, pushing the bin to the side and removing the panel. The itch in my throat grew even more, my hands shook and the guilt I felt dawned on me as I reached inside a small crevice. The hole was just large enough for me to fit my hand in and pull out a small green glass bottle. There it was. The medicine to soothe everything I felt. I unscrewed the white cap and drank allowing the bitter liquid to burn my throat slightly.

Gin was the medicine of choice today. Not that it mattered much; usually it was whatever I could afford at the time, coupled with the value and alcohol percentage. For example, one day I could buy a litre of Gordons because it was on offer in my local Tesco and then the next, I'd be gulping down a small bottle of Glen's Vodka because that's all the off-license had that was over 35% proof. Keeping it a secret became easier and easier as I became more creative with hiding places, only buying bottles that I could decant into water bottles of the same size allowing me to drink on the train or buying bottles, like this one, that could fit in a small crevice behind a bin. I sat on the kitchen tile for a few minutes, taking sips occasionally until I no longer winced at the bitter taste and the burn became a gentle tingle. The feeling of numbness radiated from my feet and worked its way to my head creating a euphoric dizziness. I stood up from the kitchen floor and shakily made my way to the bathroom, bottle in hand. I felt better again. The guilt had subsided into a joke and I laughed quietly. In the bathroom, I stood for a minute, letting wave after wave of euphoria wash over me, placing the bottle on the floor. I removed my clothes and turned the taps allowing water to hit the bottom of the bath-tub. Instinctively, I locked the door behind me and sank into the ceramic basin, letting the water fill up around me. The sound of falling water muffled the outside slightly and that's when I began to close my eyes. The alcohol had begun to take effect and I pulled the bottle from the floor and into the bath with me, drinking slower this time.

"Hello?" a voice called out, I jolted from my position, frantically placing the bottle beside me and turning the taps to stop the water. The muffled sounds of footsteps climbed the stairs and I could feel my heart beat faster as I sat still, frozen in my position. The bathroom door shook slightly, "You in there?" the voice asked, and he was home. "Do you want a cuppa love?" he asked.

"Please, I'll be down in a minute," I lied. The sound of footsteps receded back down and I receded back into the water.

# Chapter 2
## *Track 2 - Bjork - Unravel*

You have to be always drunk. That's all there is to it—it's the only way. So as not to feel the horrible burden of time that breaks your back and bends you to the earth, you have to be continually drunk. But on what? Wine, poetry or virtue, as you wish. But be drunk.

And if sometimes, on the steps of a palace or the green grass of a ditch, in the mournful solitude of your room, you wake again, drunkenness already diminishing or gone, ask the wind, the wave, the star, the bird, the clock, everything that is flying, everything that is groaning, everything that is rolling, everything that is singing, everything that is speaking...ask what time it is and wind, wave, star, bird, clock will answer you: "It is time to be drunk!" So as not to be the martyred slaves of time, be drunk, be continually drunk! On wine, on poetry or on virtue as you wish.

*Get Drunk, Charles Baudelaire*

Chris and I had been together going on two years. Our relationship was textbook good, he loved me and I loved him. It's easy to sit and analyse my actions, saying that there is no way I could've loved him, between drinking and the abhorrent infidelity it's hard to believe it myself, but I did. There was something inside of me that couldn't let him go, I couldn't tell him everything either. As far as I knew my drinking wasn't affecting our relationship too negatively, unless you count the fact that I found it hard to remember most of our conversations. The next morning my eyes slowly pried themselves open, the stale copper taste lingering in my mouth as I sighed deeply. The back of his head slowly came into focus; his mousy brown hair seemed to lift me in the morning. When your life is overrun by addiction, it's amazing what your eyes or your nose or mouth can find solace in. The smell of bacon cooking in the morning, the cheeky smile Chris gave when he told a joke that wasn't really funny, the fish swimming in the tank between the kitchen and the dining room; they all made me feel like I was comfortable. Without realising I had created a strong network of comfort. The back of his head in the morning was one of them.

The answer is always yes. To every question you ask yourself every morning, the answer is always yes. Whether or not you realise it at the time, even it feels like a no, you will always reply, yes. Do I want to live this lifestyle? *No.* Will I drink today? *No.* Will I still hold that grudge against that one person? *No.* Am I going to be completely shut off and pessimistic today? *No.* These are things I said to myself every morning but the answer was always yes. The word held so much potential to be turned around and used positively and to aid me when I needed it most. It was this word that kept me clinging on and hoping for something else or some kind of reward. Am I going to stay positive today? *Yes.* Will I stay sober today? *Yes.* Can I let small things go and not worry? *Yes.* Will I stay comfortable and continue living this way? *Yes.* So, you see, it wasn't that the answer was always yes, it needed to be.

Once again coffee proved its necessity to me, meagrely climbing over Chris to reach the bedroom door. He moved slightly. I stopped, looking back to see if I had disturbed him. I hadn't. I moved towards the bathroom across the hall, letting myself in and instinctively locking the door behind me. As I stared at myself in the mirror, I noticed that my eyes were burning red and my skin had become paler. I resembled a blood splattered sheet and felt the same. My eyes looked like a match that had just been extinguished with ashy circles surrounding a red ember. Right there staring back at me was everything I wasn't sure of. What exactly did I see? A boy, about five feet and nine inches tall, pale skin and dark hair that's kept purposefully longer on top than at the sides; his name is James.

I turned my head towards the toilet and the previous night slowly seeped through. I fell to my knees and extended my arm around the porcelain base where a gap no wider than four inches lived. My fingers felt for the cold glass of the bottle I had left there and pulled it towards my face. The plastic cap was half on and there was still some gin left in the bottom. I must've stopped myself when I got out of the bath to join Chris the previous night. As if it were an automatic response, I limply twisted the cap off and finished the bottle. An enormous amount of pressure swelled in my head as the stale copper taste was encompassed by the bittersweet flavour of gin. My body slumped on the floor as I placed the bottle between my knees. I kept my eyes closed for a moment, silent, listening. Today the answer would be yes, I lied to myself. Every other thought that stumbled through my head momentarily subsided and allowed me to feel the cold tile of my bathroom floor with more compassion than before. It was comfortable; it made the world stop spinning, just for a second.

My silent reverie subsided in an instant as I unsteadily rose to my feet. I carried the bottle loosely in my palm, carefully pressing my head against the bathroom door. I was listening for any sign of movement, nothing. I turned back on my heels, my bare feet slapping the tile and flushed the empty toilet grinning slightly. The door lock was stiff and loudly clicked as I opened the door and left the bathroom, bottle in hand, immediately heading for the stairs all the while looking in the direction of the bedroom. My eyes stayed fixed on the closed door as I continued down the stairs.

The second my feet lifted from the final step, my head began to fill with cloudy euphoria and I moved toward the kitchen, floating almost. The kitchens comfortable warmth greeted me as my eyes adjusted to a light orange glow that trickled through the window. I wrapped the bottle in kitchen roll and pushed it to the bottom of the bin. Simultaneously, I switched the kettle on and let it boil. Above the kettle, there sat a generic wood veneer set of cabinets and inside those there was a ceramic flower pot that I sometime hid money in, for emergencies. The cabinets didn't reach the ceiling, leaving a considerably sized ledge on top. As the kettle bubbled wildly and the steam flowed from the spout, I stretched my arm above my head so that my fingers could just curl above the top. I felt the ledge length ways until my fingers felt a small, rectangular packet. I grasped it in my palms and brought it down to the counter top as the kettle clicked. I opened the packet and silently counted the number of cigarettes left inside, five. Chris didn't know, I knew about these ones, he called them emergencies. The two had now become synonymous. If ever he would go out in the night, he would call them emergencies; he would ask if I had any or wanted any, all the while substituting this word for what they were. He was supposed to be cutting down; with every new packet we would open he would declare them as his last. It didn't bother me; I mean we both had secrets. I ushered myself through the living room, grabbing a stray lighter from an end table by the sofa as I passed and left through the sliding doors that sat adjacent to the stairs. As my bare feet met with the concrete floor, the sound of birds broke the silence and I closed the door behind me. I was stood on our small balcony with a communal garden below, empty and lifeless. I could see the city in the distance with the gherkin on the horizon as the sound of police sirens eclipsed my ears.

I placed a cigarette between my teeth, held it there for a second and then lit it, inhaling deeply as I let the ashy taste fill my lungs. You've heard this all before, you've heard that 'it's a metaphor' right? Well this was not a metaphor, it was a fucking cigarette. I couldn't stand the idea of being another one of these dissociative teenagers, the kind in the films that develop a terminal illness, fall in love and die. I wanted more than the straight, white protagonists who by definition are assholes. I didn't want my life to be nothing more than a pretentious title that doesn't mean anything yet somehow fools an entire generation into believing they've had a deep and spiritual connection with literature. But that's what was happening. Then again 'to kill a mockingbird' would just be called 'Black Man faces extreme prejudice from a racist society' and let's face it, not much has changed in the past sixty years. I needed to allow myself to be more honest and realise that sometimes there wasn't a deeper meaning behind things and that sometimes things just are exactly as they seem. I understand the irony in all of this, I do. I am a villain for over analysis and by no means am I saying that throwing metaphorical drivel at people is damaging but it's difficult for me to keep up with. I would have felt so much more content if everyone could pop a Valium or two and let go of all the unnecessary angst. I was drinking because I felt like it and I was smoking because that's what drinking made me feel like doing. I inhaled the last of the tobacco and threw the cigarette filter over the edge.

An hour passed by as I lay on the sofa, nursing my coffee. By this point, my legs had become numb from the alcohol induced elation that had fully set in. Chris still hadn't surfaced, so I was free to let the drink take control. All that really meant was that I could eat the entire contents of my fridge, snack unreasonable amounts for this time of morning and have no one question me on it. It also meant that I was able to re-watch episodes of Buffy the Vampire slayer and aggressively hum along to the theme tune and not have to explain what's going on. If you've ever seen it, you'd understand what a hard task that would be to someone jumping into the middle of season 6. "Why is she invisible now? Is that a power she has? I thought her job was killing monsters. Why is she at McDonalds?" and so on and so forth until I try to remove my ear drums with a pair of rusty tweezers. Silence is, in fact, golden…sometimes.

The combined haze of the previous night and this morning's lapse made me feel drowsy yet I couldn't sleep. I heard his feet on the bedroom floor above me and immediately jolted upright. His routine never faltered, he was a creature of habit and I could rely on that, as I expected, he went into the bathroom. After a few minutes, I heard the toilet flush. Then he moved into the bedroom (presumably to change) before jogging down the stairs. Every morning was the same. This worked in my favour.

He joined me in the living room and gently kissed me on the mouth. He held his face close to mine for a moment, his mousy blonde hair was dishevelled and his stubble was uncouth. His masculine ruggedness was complemented by his Nordic features and medium build. "Morning!" he whispered, his voice croaky from having just woken up, "have you brushed your teeth yet?" He winced playfully. I just flashed my empty coffee cup.

"It is the morning, I say that, it's just past eleven but you know what I mean," the combination of cigarette smoke, coffee and stale alcohol was enough to pass as common morning breath. He smiled and moved into the kitchen and I heard the kettle click, another part of his routine; a cup of tea, milk and no sugar. He called into me and predictably asked if I wanted one. I refused.

"Are you not at work today then?" he asked.

"I've got the day off, I did mention it yesterday…I think," I replied, trying to keep my words as steady as possible. Pausing the TV, I listened for anything else that he might have to say as he shuffled though holding his mug close to his face before sitting opposite me. The menial conversation continued back and forth for a few minutes, he mentioned his work for the day and I said I had nothing planned. "My new office chair is being delivered today listen out for the door please," he said before moving from his seat.

"Will I have to sign for it?"

"Of course, you will, have you never had anything delivered before?" he retorted. I didn't reply. He finished his tea and continued his morning blissfully unaware of my state.

Mid-afternoon came around and Chris had started work, leaving me to occupy myself whatever way I saw fit. He worked from home, mostly web coding for various clients and running his own freelance business. I began to sober up and my hands started to shake again and that's when I heard the sound of my phone vibrate. I hadn't even looked at it since I left work the day before, mostly, out of fear and the possibility of resurfacing guilt. I glanced at the screen and saw a name, John. I had forgotten about him and being reminded wasn't an issue at this point. Chris continued working upstairs and I hadn't moved from my spot since the morning, by this point, I had sat through three more episodes. I thought about it for a second, hesitatingly unlocking my phone and read the message. It read:

*"Hi, how are you? I've just come back from my trip to Spain and cleared out the duty free lol, fancy popping over?"*

John was a fairly wealthy man, in his thirties, who had begun talking to me when I was at work about 6 months ago. He had a home on the coast of Spain and a flat not too far from mine to which he would invite me over countless times so we could drink, so that I could drink for free. I hadn't heard from him in over a month but the last time I had seen him, he offered me a job being his assistant and I politely refused on the grounds that I had other things planned, this was a lie but I was not ready to commit to the life of Lolita. When he suggested me visiting, I knew exactly what it meant. He wanted to ply me with alcohol and allow me to act like Julia Roberts and do everything except kiss on the mouth. He was an average looking man but, in all honesty, his money took him from a possible seven to a solid nine, ten at a push. I ignored his message for a few minutes, my heart was pounding as I debated whether or not I could live with more guilt and as I thought about what seeing him would mean my stomach began to tie itself in knots. My hands began to shake and my throat began to itch. Before I knew it, I had typed out a reply:

*"I can't stay for long, I'll just hop on the train and be over in five, see you soon."*

I hit send. I felt a lump in my throat, as if it weren't me who had control over my hands or even my feet as I marched up the stairs and threw on a knitted jumper and some jeans. He had previously commented on this outfit before, so it only seemed fair. The drink was taking over again; it was the Jekyll to my Mr. Hyde, the Hulk to my Bruce Banner, and Gollum to my Sméagol. I told Chris I was going for a walk and would probably do some shopping on the way back; he accepted this without hesitation, kissing me before I finally left to catch the bus.

The problem I faced day to day was that I lacked the contrariety to care; I lacked the moral compass to point me south when I got lost in the haze. Everything was casual, nothing had a sense of urgency or importance and nothing became prevalent in my behaviour that made me stop and think: I am in trouble.

# Chapter 3
## *Track 3 – Azure Ray*
## *– Displaced*

Sometimes things can't exist in the absence of something else. Love exists in the absence of hate, happiness and joy exists in the absence of sadness and anger. We feel hot because it's not cold and freeze in the absence of heat. The list goes on. I exist in the absence of sobriety and in the absence of inebriation. I coexist with all the possibilities in the absence of everything else. I feel hate and love in the absence of the nothingness that feels my head in a sober stupor. Think about everything you have and everything you live with and without. I imagine the things you live without outweigh the things you live with, of course it does, nobody has everything. Even if you have a lot or more than the average person, there is an equal and opposite to everything you have, the thing that allows you to have what you do in its absence. Chris and I existed because of each other, he was peace and I was chaos. He was love and I was hate and because neither of us had the opposite, we lived together in spite of each other. He allowed me to live in peace in spite of the fact that I cause the most chaos in his life, even if he didn't know it yet.

Day to day, Chris didn't have a single hateful bone in his body, none that he was aware of anyway, I gave him that; I gave him the anger and passion in the form of senseless arguments and exaggerated sarcasm. In return, I received love and peace of mind, a fair trade in any book. I thought of all the possibilities and I thought about everything that I had and that I could be, because I lived without other aspects of a normal life. I thought forwards and backwards and up and down and I thought every way possible as I lay half naked on the floor of Johns' apartment. I looked around the room, modern and minimal with a large TV mounted on one wall surrounded by various pieces of art. A large king-sized bed sat behind me and everything was either black or white. I reached for the glass that had been left for me, all the while allowing the regret and disdain within myself build up. The taste of vodka and coke hit the back of my throat and my mind fogged up for a few minutes. I felt everything and nothing at the same time. I felt raw guilt that somehow melted into hysterical comedy. My clothes were strewn somewhere closer to the bed and with a gentle push I moved to my feet. Stumbling I reached for the pack of cigarettes that sat on his bedside table with only my underwear to hide my modesty.

Time had no meaning here. Time was dangerous and humbled by my presence there. It had me moving forward and backwards all at the same time not allowing me to have any grasp on the harsh reality of the situation.

John had gotten in the shower and I could hear the water running from across the hallway so I knew it was my time to leave. I had gotten everything I wanted and I had used him for all I could at this present moment. I took one large gulp of my drink, finishing it in one go as I searched the table for a lighter. I opened the top draw of the table, moving various different papers to the side, lightly glancing at them picking and choosing the information to take in. Bank statements with numbers on that I couldn't even count to on, prescriptions for numerous medications, some I recognised and finally the letter that stopped me in my tracks; a letter from the CSA outlining child support payments. Money was no object for this man, I could see that from the five digits that were printed at the bottom of the bank note, but his house bared no remanence of children ever having occupied the space. Beneath that, I finally found the lighter next to a box of Tramadol. I lit my cigarette and pulled the letter closer to my face, reading in more depth than I should have. Apparently, he had two children, both only a few years younger than myself. I felt sick. Instinctively, I held the cigarette between my teeth, unscrewed the vodka bottle that sat on the floor where I had just been laying and took a long sip. I slouched on the bed slowly smoking and threw the letter back in the draw, holding the vodka between my legs. All I had were questions and thoughts and time. Why had he not mentioned them before? Was he just as disgusted with himself as I now was? Besides that, how did a thirty-year-old man who's low-key shagging me have two children of early adolescents? As I began to slide the draw shut, I noticed the pills again. I slipped the foil packet from the box, it was untouched and clean. I removed two and swallowed them down. Without hesitation, I grabbed them from the box and shut the rest in the draw, quickly pulling my jeans on putting them in my pocket as I did so. I hauled on the rest of my clothes, all the while smoking and drinking before hearing the click of the bathroom door.

"You going somewhere?" he said, with a cheeky smile, drying himself and entering the bedroom. It was different than before; he closed the door and now for some reason the room felt emptier. My guilt had somehow erased him as I knew him and replaced him with a rich single father who was so far in the closet that he was still deciding what he should wear to work three years ago. In that moment, my life turned into an episode of sex and the city and somehow it was gayer. He stepped closer, drying himself all the while holding his smile. He stood there, a little taller than me, brown hair perfectly quaffed and trimmed at the sides still damp from his shower. His bathrobe was slightly looser at the top, revealing his tanned pecs. For a dad, he was well put together, he frequented the gym and obviously looked after himself; I mean if it wasn't for the two teenagers, he could've easily passed for twenty-nine. His deep, husky voice was like smoke that filled my lungs and I simply replied with a smile and a nod as I pulled my shoes on.

"This…can't happen again," I slurred my words slightly, finishing my cigarette and placing it in the ashtray to the side. He placed a cigarette in his mouth before lighting it and staring at me confused, pushing passed me and sitting on the

31

bed. Fully clothed I stood in the doorway and held the vodka in my hand, swigging it before mustering up the courage to speak; "I'm going to leave now and I probably won't see you for a while, okay? Okay. Good."

"What are you talking about?" he inhaled, widening his legs slightly, revealing his nakedness beneath his robes,

"You put that away, I'm serious!" I snapped back, stepping over to him standing a few inches away from the bed, my head became cloudy again and I felt oddly dizzy. He smiled again and moved his hands up the length of my jeans stopping at the crotch, softly rubbing whilst holding his cigarette to one side. I smiled back and ran my fingers through his hair. He moved his head forward stopping to unzip my jeans as I grabbed the cigarette from his hand placing a kiss on his cheek.

"Goodbye John!" I grinned, turning and leaving his apartment. I made the executive decision to tackle one problem at a time. After seeing John for who he was and what he wanted from me, it was as if that bottle of vodka was the last shot of courage I needed. Of course, I left the apartment with the alcohol and the stolen pills but I was making a step in the right direction, home.

Besides, the next day, I had to re-join society as an active member of the contributing hive. In doing so, I would re-immerse myself into reality hard and with great gravity this time with no escape. For the sake of continuity, I picked up a one-pound pizza from Iceland and a bag of frozen chips, an effortless attempt at what I would later call dinner. When I arrived home, I told Chris that I didn't feel well and slipped the vodka into my work bag. He tried to make conversation about his new chair arriving and he couldn't wait to show me. His eyes would light up over the smallest of things and they held so much passion and life I felt grateful to be a part of. It made my head hurt with writhing guilt that I couldn't shake. He made me realise that it's these little things that make you realise the feelings you have for someone. It's the way you remember how they take their tea or how they like their gravy on their Sunday dinner. It's in the way you remember what dinner to make when they've had a rough day or the jokes to tell when they're upset. It's the explosive feeling of anger and joy all at the same time caused by something they've said and it's more than just being able to say 'I love you', it's being able to feel it with every fibre of your being. I felt that and I know he felt the same. The times I had betrayed these feelings weren't me, not really. I couldn't help myself and I feared that Chris couldn't either.

Apart of me felt like he knew. A tiny voice in the back of my mind, the one I usually shut up with a drink or five, would say that he knew everything. It told me he knew when I was drunk or when I'd swallowed a ton of pills to make me sleep or even when I'd slept with other people. If he did know, should I have been angry at him for allowing me to continue in the obviously self-destructing ways? Should I have felt lonely or lost when he looked at me in the way that would tell me everything was going to be ok even if it wasn't? Everything was happening all at once and my spiral of inner conflict was becoming a circle. As the day drew to a close and Chris had hit me with endless sickening positivity, I lay in bed with my thoughts and allowed the spiral to pull me down.

The next morning, I awoke to the same routine as before, the assaulting sound of my alarm, the comfort of Chris's face first thing in the morning and the bittersweet taste of coffee to mask the stale alcohol. I knew I had to march on into work, face the hive and face another challenge. I moved to the bathroom as I always did and stared into the mirror, preparing myself for the day ahead. I saw nothing unusual, the same bloodshot eyes staring out of the same blank face. Today the answer would be no, I told myself. I thought to myself that if anything should come up regarding my manager, I would say no. This day, I would stand my ground and refuse to engage with him the way he wanted me to. I would be honest today and refuse any advances like I had done with John. If I could say no to him then the possibilities were endless. As I moved towards the front door to leave, I remembered what I had slipped into my bag the previous night. I stopped. I wasn't ready yet; I could feel my hands moving before I could think about what to do. I rushed into the kitchen and searched through the cabinets to find an empty bottle of some sort. I found an old Lucozade bottle and poured in what was left of the vodka. I was ready to leave.

The commute was the same as usual; the hive swallowed me as it usually did. It pushed me and poked me into every corner it could, all the while I would take sips of what everyone would assume was Lucozade, the spirit would hit my throat and keep me floating as I travelled. I entered the shop and allowed the day of retail to unravel, all the while floating on my cloud of inebriation. Of course, my manager and I shared the occasional conversation, he asked me to re-stock and tidy whilst the shop was quiet and I would ask him to refrain from touching my thigh even though I knew he wouldn't. Even as I drank through the day, I was able to bat off his advances and I felt good about myself for what I was doing.

"We're closing together today remember?" he reminded me as he gently slapped my ass, to which I replied by pinching his left nipple. He let out a little scream followed by a giggle, he thought of it all as playful banter.

"Go and have some lunch before I call HR," I joked; he laughed and proceeded to exit the shop floor. I would never do that. I knew I was just as much to blame as he was in all of this, but in times like this it helped to remind him where we stood, even if it meant nothing. I turned to face the shelves behind the counter where I stood, continuing with my work. The shop was eerily silent and the fluorescent lights clouded my vision slightly. The vodka was beginning to wear off. I reached for Lucozade bottle I had left on the counter top, it was empty.

"Hello you!" a deep, husky voice trickled through the empty space and made me look up, it was John. He stood on the opposite side of the counter, he smelled of Hugo Boss fragrance and his hair was perfectly shaped. The lights outlined his cheek bones and his blue eyes sparkled slightly.

"What are you doing here?" I said blankly, the sobriety was seeping into me and I was beginning to feel sick,

"Charming, after yesterday, you just left me a little hungry is all."

"You're repugnant, go away please. I'm far too busy trying to think of better things to do," my voice trembled slightly as I tried to assert a sardonic a tone as possible. My mind filled with too many thoughts, all of which involved me either jumping in front of a bus or allowing him to jump my bones for the sake of some peace and quiet. "You can't be here," I whispered, "I'll take a break in five minutes just go round the corner and wait for me," I finished, looking over my shoulder for any signs of my manager. He smiled again and left without another word.

"He was cute!" a voice came from behind me, "Bit of a daddy though? Don't you think?" It was him. He joined me at the counter and I just laughed, refraining from swearing as he was completely right. My head became clearer and I was feeling more and more sick. Five minutes came and went and I was trying to think of the many reasons why I couldn't take a break until it dawned on me that if I didn't leave to see him, he would come back and see me. I couldn't risk that again, I was trying to get rid of these people.

I left the shop and found him standing a few feet away from some public toilets. His grin was wider than I'd ever seen it and I knew exactly what he was thinking. This was it, I thought to myself, time to say no.

"No," I said, the word came surprisingly easy to me. His smirk quickly faded. "Look, we need to stop this, I can't see you anymore and you definitely can't be coming into my place of work and think we're going to pull a Clapham Junction in a public toilet, what are you doing here anyway don't you have a job?"

"I told you, you left me yesterday and I just want more, look I bought you something." He pulled a brown paper bag from beneath his coat. Another bottle of Vodka, I thought. "You've got time, come on," he pushed, gesturing to the entrance. I thought of his children and I thought of all the surrounding public. I thought of the bottle in his hand and I took it from him.

35

"Just go!" I replied, pushing back the words I so desperately wanted to say. My mind was forcing his children out into the open, like vomit I wanted to spew his secret all over the pavement, shout at him in front of everyone and embarrass him into leaving. I couldn't. I held the bag in my hand and turned to walk away; as I did, he, grabbed me by the arm. "Just five minutes, you owe me," his voice was quieter this time, deeper and more intense. His grip was tight and as I looked into his eyes they had changed, they no longer sparkled or even resembled the same blue. I felt a sense of fear build up in the pit of my stomach as his tone became more stern and firm. Instead of running like I should have, I turned and smiled back. I shook myself from his grasp. "First of all, I need more than five minutes, you should know that by now," I joked. "Second, I owe you fuck all remember that. If I were you, I'd be more concerned of John Junior and what you owe him or them should I say?" I was suddenly empowered and he took a step backwards. He looked to the floor before taking a step closer to me, "Come over tomorrow, we can talk, I won't try anything, I promise," he begged. I stayed silent.

"Please James, let me explain," he finished, I turned back to face away from him.

"Fine, but only because you bought me a gift," I flirted, "I'll be over at 7." That was it. It was the way he said my name, it was like inhaling smoke and having it fill your lungs without burning the back of your throat. So much goes into a name, when people say it, they are saying every other person or factor that went into choosing that for you. When it all boils down to it though, it's just a sound people use to tell us apart and direct themselves towards us. But when those sounds are forced out at the right level with the right tone, it's like magic. It can make you realise just how angry someone is with you or it can make you see just how desperate they are for your help. After I left him on the street and attempted to go back to work, hiding his gift beneath my shirt, I told my manager I wasn't feeling well and went home. A part of me just wanted to avoid having to deal with him at the end of the day and the other part couldn't deal with the idea of John and the idea of having to go home to Chris and act normal.

Perhaps this was it for me, I thought. Maybe everyone I knew felt this way and maybe everyone I had ever come into contact with had the same thoughts and trials to deal with. I had been so wrapped up in my own self-loathing that I had neglected to even think about everyone else involved. Perhaps, people in the middle-ages felt like this when they thought they'd sold their souls to the devil. It was a curious, exhilarating, not unpleasant sensation, but at the same time, I felt so scared. I was terrified of what I was capable of and what I was doing and who I was doing it to. Yes, I said to myself, I've done it now. I am lost.

# Chapter 4

## Track 4 – Aimee Mann – Invisible Ink

There's something about early winter mornings that somehow radiate a sense of nostalgia. The crisp air fills your nose and gives you a feeling of longing for something that doesn't even exist. I stood in the street and let the cold take me somewhere new, somewhere different. Even if everything around me reeked of the now, I would see a man with a tattooed face begging for change or see some children kicking the life out of another child for looking at them wrong and I would still feel a sense of winter's disposition. This is England, I thought; fuck the tea parties and fish and chip Fridays, it was all about the drug addled yobs that ruled the streets in minus temperatures. I stood there and realised that you can take the 'BNP' and the 'Lib Dems' and see that they're all fighting for the same thing. They're fighting for the right to be British as that's a quintessentially good thing; as if the streets weren't littered with born and bred fuck-wits who now epitomised 'being British'. I also realised regardless of everything, the winter mornings still instilled a sense of wonder and the local corner shop still welcomed you like family and every week you'd see something that would make you stop and think 'This is good'. I saw these things in every day that would make me want to be good, I would ask every morning 'please make me good for something other than this'. Looking back, I'm unsure exactly who I was supposed to be asking, but I guess it was good to verbalise.

This was the beginning of the end, I thought. This was the 'beginning' of the change I needed. I could not let everything come full circle this time. As I shuffled along the pavement to reach the train station, the cold penetrated my body. I was going to John's to tell him the truth and hopefully put a stop to the madness and try to fix things for myself. Chris would never know and I could move forwards. I had tactfully waited until the next morning to go to his apartment, this way Chris would just think I was going to work and I wouldn't have to make any excuses like I would have if I had decided to go the evening before. I even made an extra effort to adorn a large coat coupled with a belt that was particularly difficult to remove. Accompanied by my usual work bag, this time with an empty Lucozade bottle and the gift John had given me. I planned to return the vodka in an effort to show that I couldn't be bought, a refund of sorts. The streets were icy and my boots struggled to keep a firm grip as I approached the station.

Just before the station, on the cold ground, I saw a woman crying and begging passers-by for change. Her top lip was swollen and her bottom jaw was swinging from side to side between breaths as she cried out for help. Instantly my mind jumped to the thought of the come down she was clearly experiencing. As more people ignored her, she began smacking the side of her face repeatedly, crying harder than before. I too passed her by. After that, I saw another woman in front of the station entrance handing out leaflets emblazoned with the words: *'Let the Lord In'*. I ignored her too. She ought to have handed one to the drug riddled woman and see what the lord could find in her. This is my England, I thought.

I arrived at his apartment soon after and approached the door cautiously. My mind was telling me to leave the vodka on the doorstep and run, it would've been sort of poetic that way. No more words just an unwanted gift and a see you later. Although in that respect, I may as well have never gone over and kept the gift, he'd never know either way. I slipped my hand into my bag and grabbed at the bottle, pulling it out. I stopped. My hesitant hands held it by my side for a second, contemplating whether or not to let it go, but before I could make a decision, the door clicked and my arm retracted upwards. I had no choice, he was stood in front of me as I held the bottle in my hands. He stood in the doorway, wearing his signature robes and nothing else.

"Ah Fuck!" I said aloud before I could stop myself, he looked confused for a second before it melted into the charming smile he relied on. I just smiled back and pushed passed him, avoiding eye contact or any contact for that matter. I moved into his bedroom and consciously kept my coat on. I held on to the bottle and nothing was said between us as he closed his door and moved to join me. I placed the bottle on the floor, opening my coat slightly, breathing deep, "You have two children, my age or there about," I said with a sigh of relief. He looked hurt almost, as if I had said something to wound him and his ego.

"This can't go on, I have a boyfriend who I live with and you're just some man who has money. We can't keep this going," I continued. He looked to the floor.

"We need to talk," he said softly, grazing my arm with his hand,

"We really don't." I retorted, shrugging his grasp moving towards the door. I wanted that to be it, for me to just say what I needed to and leave.

"This isn't just about you, as much as you'd like it to be," he replied, the words made me shake a little. How he could think I was only thinking about myself, I thought. He had children of a similar age to me and I couldn't ignore that regardless of how much money he had or how nice his apartment was. He grabbed my arm once more, locking my eyes with his. "You spoke. I listened. Time for me to leave," I said with as stern a voice as I could muster, his hands still holding my arm tight.

"I'm sorry." He said softly, his tone reverberated with sincerity as I pulled away from his grasp once more. He thought I was angry and hurt by what had happened but I was relieved by the opportunity to give it a rest. "Not that it matters now. But I needed you to know that," he uttered his words dejectedly, all the while I stood frozen in the doorway.

I was between paths. I could have turned and walked out of the door and never returned, but my feet were frozen.

"Why?"

"Because I care about you!"

"Then you might want to try not having children of my age and letting us do this, I mean, I'm young enough to be your son, we could've been friends in school, and doesn't that make you think at all?" I was lying to myself, I didn't care about any of this and I didn't need an explanation. There was just a little voice in the back of my mind telling me to fight my corner, act as if I were hurt and milk it somehow.

"It's different, you're different," he whispered, his hands were now firmly at his side and I remained in the doorway, keeping my distance, "You could've stopped all of this when we met, you knew who I was and you didn't," he continued. "The same to you!" I shouted, "I couldn't!" I finished, my anger rising.

"Because you loved me," he whispered. My eyes widened and my mouth turned as I listened to the words that poured from his mouth. I realised that it was too late for any retribution no matter how charming his smile. I softly spoke "No. I don't!" The minute I spoke the words his face seemed to change. The words cut him like a knife and I was the blade. In that moment I could see everything he thought we were but we were nothing.

"Why do you keep lying to yourself?" he whispered.

"I'm not saying I don't have feelings for you. I do. But it's not love. I could never trust you enough for it. You're trying to build something with a person who barely saw the fall of VHS against DVD when you sat and listened to Vinyl's as a teenager," I countered. My feet moved before I could think and I was left stood a few inches in front of his half-dressed body.

"Trust is for old married couples, James. I've been there, got the child support payments to prove it, what we have is wild and passionate and dangerous and it consumes me."

"Calm the fuck down Shakespeare, you're talking about something that takes over our lives and I have had enough of

41

that!" I screamed. By this point, I was angry and his passion burned through his eyes as I stood only a few inches from him. He moved towards me, desperate, like a tortured animal begging for forgiveness.

"I know you feel like I do. You don't have to hide it anymore," he moved to kiss me. I gently tried to stop him, waving my arm to push his aside.

"John, stop it!" I turned my head and my feet continued to be rooted to the floor.

"Let yourself feel it." He whispered as he kissed my neck, becoming more forceful.

"Stop it, you're crazy!" I said, as it escalated quickly and I found myself in a very real struggle.

"You love me!" he kept repeating the words in an effort to make them truer, forcefully kissing my neck as he pushed.

"Stop!" I said finally, batting his face away from mine. I stumbled back, losing my balance I grabbed onto the door handle, falling. The handle slipped from my grasp as I fell to the floor like debris from a bomb. My head cracked against the edge of his bedside table making me stumble even more. It took me a few seconds to come to my senses. It was an accident, I thought. He was on me, oblivious to my pain, kissing me more forcefully than before. "Let it go. Let yourself love me!" he whispered, kissing me all over, "Stop it. Please, stop!" I said as he whispered, trying to overcome his deep tones with my weak voice. He didn't listen. I struggled with him, pain shooting through my skull as he lay on top of me, desperate, hungry.

He continued to touch me and kissed me on my neck, "I know you felt it. When I was inside you."

"STOP!" I cried as tears began to form in my eyes. I managed to push him off and scuttled for the door like a wounded animal. He caught my leg, scrambling back on top of me and pinning my wrists down. I could smell his carpet as it began burning my face with friction.

"You're going to let me inside you," he said firmly, his charm had burned away.

"Please." I whispered.

"You'll feel it again, James!" he was determined; he was like an animal unleashed for the hunt. No longer would his eyes burn a bright blue, they would forever be filled with an evil I had never faced. "John, stop!" I pleaded, He tore at my coat and pulled my jeans down. I could see my bag sat a few feet away from our position on the floor. The bottle of vodka sat graciously beside it.

"I'll make you feel it," he whispered.

"STOP!" I shoved him back, exploding with rage. Tears ran down my face and my fingers grabbed at the base of the bottle. As my fingers wrapped around the cold glass, I felt the anger that surged through me and felt his skin against mine. Adrenaline coursed through me as I pulled the bottle above my head and struck him as hard as I could across the face. He jumped to the side, smashing against the opposite wall, cracking the plaster and crashing to the floor. I struggled to my feet, trembling with rage and fear, the bottle in hand. With one swift movement, I removed the cap and drank from the bottle.

"Ask me again why I could never love you," I said, on my feet with the bottle in hand, breathing heavy. A drop of blood fell from his brow as he struggled to regain balance; before he could rise to his feet I kicked him, knocking him back down. I looked at his unconscious body and began to cry. The tears came from my eyes almost instinctively as I fell to my knees. Immediately, I wiped my face, grasping at my bag, removing the empty bottle I was carrying with me. The bottle I held in my hand acted as a painkiller, instantly I felt better as I drank. My hands were shaking as I decanted it from the glass bottle to the plastic Lucozade one I had carried with me. Of all the ways the scenario had played put in my mind, this was not one of them. I had imagined we would talk about his children and I would leave the bottle and walk away, at the very least he would guilt me into one last blowjob, but not this. I stood in the doorway for a few seconds, looking at the floor where he lay unconscious.

Instantly my tears stopped as I took a sip from the bottle. I stared at him for a while as his body didn't twitch, I wanted to check to see if he was alive but in all honesty I didn't care. I moved to his bedside table pulling the draw out and filling my pockets with pills. His wallet sat on the side and without thinking, I grabbed what I could from there, all the notes and change, around fifty pounds in total. I was disgusted with the both of us, I felt nothing. I left the empty glass bottle on the floor by his side; people would think he had drank himself into that state and fell over, I thought to myself. I left without looking back. When he awoke, if he did, I would never have to have contact with him again.

The vodka began to fill my mind and I began to feel the sting of inebriation once more. I couldn't tell anyone without explaining what had happened and I couldn't do that without destroying myself. I was alone, lost once more. I moved down the corridor of his building as I left his apartment and made my way to the train station as fast as I could.

A few minutes later, as I was moving towards the train, my lips become dry and my throat began to itch. My bag knocked against my knees and I could hear the sound of liquid hitting the sides of the bottle. As I continued to edge myself on to the platform, I slid my hand into my bag carefully; as though I was revealing everything in front of the hundreds of people that surrounded me. I pulled out the Lucozade bottle that I had filled earlier and took a sip. Then another two, the taste of the white spirit soothed the itch as my head became cloudy and forgetful.

I stood on the platform, waiting for the train, when I noticed a child no older than two or three. He was surrounded by his perfectly nuclear family and was holding something in his hands making unintelligible noise, as children do. As I looked closer, I noticed that he was playing with two plastic Pac-man ghosts, the orange and blue to be exact. I continued staring that them, lost in my own thoughts until I awkwardly made eye contact with the mother. I smiled at her and averted my eyes back to the track.

Everything was eerily quiet; it was if London had decided to sleep, as if it wanted me to listen and see more than usual. The hush was soon broken by the sound of plastic hitting hard against concrete floor, my head jerked downward following the noise. My eyes met with the blue ghost as it bounced passed my foot and in almost perfect synchronicity with another approaching train, fell onto the tracks. I could hear the mother explain to the boy that what he had done was silly and that even though he wanted to, he could never get his toy back. The child didn't seem to care and carried on.

How easy would it be to become the blue ghost? Wait for another approaching train and just take a few more steps. How easy would it be to say yes to this? Say yes to another impulse and with perfect timing merge with the tracks. It couldn't have been more than four or five steps until I'd be there. I looked to the schedule above my head; 3 minutes. Before I could even think my feet had moved across the painted yellow line on the concrete. It would've taken another few inches at the most. Like an automatic reaction I took another sip from the bottle I had ignorantly left in my hand. I heard it again. The sound of plastic hit the concrete once more as the time table changed above my head. 'Stand Back, Train Approaching', the sign read. I looked towards my feet again as the orange ghost rolled by, almost in slow motion this time. Without thinking, I stretched out my leg and stopped the toy centimetres before the tracks, my foot almost balancing on the edge. The train rushed by, inches from my face as I bent down and picked up the ghost, handing it directly to the mother who thanked me; I just smiled. It was that easy to stop it. It was that easy to decide. I could have let the toy roll on to the tracks and be crushed like the one before; but I didn't. It was that easy to allow myself some respite and stay on the platform. I boarded the train.

# Chapter 5
## Track 5 - Sneaker Pimps
## - 6 Overground

The Oxford dictionary defines alcohol as a *'colourless, volatile, flammable liquid which is produced by the natural fermentation of sugars and is the intoxicating constituent of wine, beer, spirits and other drinks'*. Our bodies are slaves to old sugar. That's all it is, old, fermented sugar and yeast, a mouldy piece of bread by another name. So why does it control some of us? Is it that the sugar is just too sweet for some of us? Does the yeast rise to our heads and grow something new that we feel like we can't live without? Is it all of the above? For me, I didn't like being sober. Sometimes I would wake up with a feeling of doubt or dread that I would in fact have to face the day like a normal human being and that frightened me. Alcohol made everything fuzzy and warm, it turned hate into laughter, embarrassment into a joke and sex into love. It allowed me to frolic in the glory and buckle in the shame with no regrets whatsoever. Alcohol allowed me to see my world and not care one bit that the whole thing was collapsing around me. I guess, like everything, it's a matter of perspective.

Trouble seems to find me wherever I go; it's as if the universe is constantly reminding me that no matter how hard I try, there will always be something to stop me. I mean, all my life, I have done nothing to attract the attention of older men or anyone for that matter and yet they always find me. I have never actually actively sought out the plethora of men who want nothing more from me than what my mouth has to offer (and I'm not talking about my sparkling personality and dazzling wit). What is it about gay men, or men in general, that grow up with a sense of entitlement that makes them think they are owed a blow job by anyone who smiles politely and gives them the time of day? Why must they insist on flexing their erections through their trousers in the most inconvenient of places? Reality must share some space in their heads and tell them that calling it an anaconda when it's nothing more than an earthworm is not a turn on, it's violating. Remember, however, if you do sleep with these men you are a whore. These men lurk around every corner and follow me in everything I do, they're like sex gremlins that set their prying eyes on my prepubescent looking face and pounce. I'm clearly at fault though, my oversized jumpers and skinny jeans are too revealing and I'm obviously asking for it.

I was making light of a situation that could have otherwise destroyed everything I was working towards. Maybe, I actually did search for trouble and maybe, I did in some twisted way, enjoy the attention I could only otherwise receive as a street walker. When I arrived home, I acted as if nothing had happened. Chris was wrapped up in his new office chair as the box filled half the space in the spare room. The thought had never occurred to me that he needed to know. I stumbled through the front door and removed my bag, leaving it in the doorway. He hated that.

As I entered the house, the smell of air freshener assaulted my nose and I could see dirty dishes piled high in the kitchen. It was dark outside and I had held up the charade of being at work all day; I was angry. I was angry at myself and Chris was to get the brunt of it. Addiction is an illness, except the people that are affected expand further than yourself, the illness reaches past you and ends every relationship you had with everyone. I stormed through the house and rushed up the stairs, entering the spare room where Chris was working. I saw him sat at his computer; the room was warm and familiar, immediately, I sat on the bed. He looked at me knowingly and my mind started to race, by this point, the alcohol had taken its toll and my body began to sway back and forth. He knew. He knew something was wrong and his eyes told me all I needed to know. An awkward silence hung in the air for a few moments as I tried to focus my eyes on his. With all the uncountable times I had been this way and he'd have no idea, this was to be the time that gave the game away. That's all this was to me; a game. In my head, I couldn't define a time when it stopped being fun and started being less about winning. As an addict, you'd never know what was new or different. To those of us who have allowed the addiction to be a part of us, the outside world has no clue as to what's going on inside our heads. You allow yourself respite on sober days by comparing yourself to others, filling your time with pop culture and people that portrayed what you are going through in larger extremes. What's another day with the idea of anonymity in mind? It was like listening to Claire de lune whilst beating someone to a bloody pulp; the beauty of the noise allowed us to forgive the act itself. The gentle sound of peace let me skate through without a thought for the anarchy. Because no-one could tell I was drinking it made it ok. I was able to get through my day as a functioning human being without a single person realising that I was as incoherent as Sylvester Stallone on crack.

"How was your day?" He asked, looking to his computer screen, my mouth hung open as I tried to steady myself on the end of the bed. I just nodded and stuttered out a few meagre words. His tone didn't shift, he was either clueless or ignorant and at this point, I was unsure what was worse. I forced a smile and as I did, I could feel my mood elevate, as if I'd flicked a switch and everything was OK. The anger and confusion that I felt as I walked through the door melted away. His computer screen went black as he pressed at his keyboard and turned in his seat. The black leather squealed and the hinges creaked; I became nervous. He looked me dead in the eye as he leant forward and took my hand in his. This was it, I thought. He knew and he was about to tell me some horrific news that he could no longer stay with me and that the drink was obviously more important than our relationship and I needed to work on it all alone.

"I know," he began, sighing heavily, I stayed silent. "I know I've been a bit distant lately, with work and everything," he said. I took a deep breath and concealed my joy. I looked down play-acting to his words, pretending it was all real. "I've been so wrapped up in this that we haven't even had time for each other, not really," he apologised, keeping hold of my hand. My head remained cloudy as I pretended to be lost for words.

"Come on, let's go out tonight. We could go see a show or have dinner or something," he said, smiling sweetly. I looked up at him and swallowed hard. "Sure, I'd like that!" I whispered, sharing his smile as he leaned in and kissed me on the mouth. I stood up from the bed, all the while holding his hands in mine. I told him I needed to get changed and to give me an hour and made my exit as steady as I was able.

Thoughts are just as powerful as words. In fact, if I think about it, a thought is worth more than words. With a single thought, a person can find strength in themselves and in their minds that they had no knowledge of. Words can be kept from verbalisation as can thoughts but whereas words can be kept from you, thoughts cannot. Your thoughts are your own, no matter what, they are a part of you and you can't hide from them. The stranger you saw on the street that you imagined naked, the ex you thought about texting or even the kebab you thought about scoffing down whilst on a diet all exist. You can't un-think them. With words you can say sorry and everything can be okay again. Some people think just because they don't action a thought that it's as if it doesn't exist, but the truth is it does. Whatever it is you thought, you thought it, no matter how vile, or painful or nasty. You thought it and it's there, so the only thing for you to do is live with it. For example, my thoughts of this day, turned to the sting of copious amounts of alcohol I was going to consume, even if I was aware that it was the wrong way to deal with the situation. Any time I drank, it was like a force that I couldn't stop. It was less glamorous than Luke Skywalker but the force had awoken within me. I couldn't stop it no matter how hard I tried and I would continue to let it take control until I couldn't any more. I started to undress; the bedroom was cold and empty and my head continued to fill with fog. As I unbuttoned my trousers, letting them fall to my ankles I caught sight of myself in the full-length mirror that stood opposite the bed. I often did this. I would stare at myself and take it all in, the pale skin, dishevelled hair and tiny drunken eyes all stared back at me. I noticed bruises on my leg which reminded me of John. My hands fell to my sides and I slowly ran my fingers across the purple skin above my knee. I would blame the marks on my natural clumsiness and no one would question it, should they be seen by anyone.

I had irrevocably painted myself into a corner with him. If I were to ever find someone else, my problems would only lay hidden again; or at least hide for another few years. I mean, my own mother had no idea or anyone I knew professionally or anyone else in my life. I had managed to don a disguise so well that it was no longer a disguise, to everyone else around me, it was who I am. It would be unfair to repeat any of this to Chris without guilting him into staying with me, basically be saying "you need to stay with me otherwise I'm just going to get worse and then that's on you," which would've been a manipulation of the worst variety; it would be just as bad as saying I'd kill myself if he were to leave. I could never do that. I had done what I had done, I'd already ruined things and now it was time to face up to it whether I liked the outcome or not; this time it wasn't about me.

I heard a gentle tap on the door, instantly turning, I saw Chris poke his head in, grinning slightly. His eyes traced my body and his smile widened. "You almost ready?" He asked, as I stood naked and let the room surround me. His eyes were wide and hungry, he looked at me naked and it felt like he couldn't resist. He leant in to kiss me and I just stood and let him. My body felt weak; we hadn't looked at each other in weeks and now he was upon me and I was so blindly drunk that I would never remember it. Is this how I wanted to rekindle the relationship? Definitely not. The burden I bore weighed upon me like cement that was setting fast; I was sinking and suffocating under it. His mouth moved down my body and I could feel his lips tenderly caress my neck. His arms jolted and flung themselves around my back, lifting my legs around his waist as my face began to burn with passion and he threw me on the bed. He was on top of me and I lay there so enamoured by his passion that every thought I had melted away; this is what love felt like. We made love for an hour and a half, kissing and stroking one another until it was over.

He pushed himself from me and started to dress, handing me a towel to clean up, "come on," he said "we need to get a move on!" I jolted from my horizontal position. I wiped myself over with toilet tissue and began to get dressed; my head was still cloudy from before, however I couldn't stop thinking about my next drink. I was dressed and ready to go as Chris brushed his teeth; I moved downstairs and headed to the kitchen. On the side sat a bottle of red wine. Instinctively, I uncorked the bottle and took a long sip. The earthy taste flooded my mouth as I reached into the cupboard for two glasses. I poured myself one and Chris half a glass; he would never notice I thought. It was his idea to go out, it was his idea to celebrate with a few drinks, even though I knew what I did, it was still all his idea.

The night drew on as we hopped from bar to bar. Gay culture in London makes sure that one drink is impossible, if you're single it's a shark tank, if you're in a couple it's even more carnivorous. A bar in Leicester Square packed to the brim with like-minded people; with nowhere to sit we stood in the courtyard smoking cigarette after cigarette. Chris had bought me a beer and we stood in the corner, hiding from the crowds. By this point my mind had completely turned to the drink and as I sipped the beer Chris had bought me. I couldn't help but think about the next. I wanted to know what was next. In a drunken stupor, I let everything go. "I'm an Alcoholic!" I said to him, in the crowded bar in the corner away from everyone as I sipped my beer. His face lit up with confusion and disbelief; "that's a lie" he told himself. For once, I was telling the truth albeit a little unconventional but for some reason, this was the turning point and he had to know. My head was completely clouded and it just felt right. The admission was strange to me, I'd never said it aloud before and I wasn't even sure if that's what this was but it sounded correct. The bar was alive with the hum of voices and clashing glasses and my voice seemed to be lost in the din.

I don't remember the journey home, I don't remember going to bed either; my eyes opened the next morning and squinted through the streams of light that forced their way into the bedroom. My arms reached out to an empty space. My mouth felt like a sand pit and tasted just as bad, there was a pressure building up inside my head as I feebly got up from my bed. Shakily making my way down stairs I could hear the sound of ceramic mugs hitting a work top accompanied by the sound of a boiling kettle. I stayed silent as I slumped on to the sofa but I could see Chris making coffee for me. My mind had forgotten about our conversation for a moment, before my mind jolted back the previous night. I felt a rush of embarrassment and shame; I wanted to crawl into a hole and pretend that nothing happened. "Fucking idiot!" I whispered to myself, not realising that he was within earshot; "what was that?" He asked, handing me a hot mug. I just smiled and shook my head, looking for the remote.

In my head, I thought of every scenario that wouldn't involve us talking about my confession, I had never felt regret like it. A part of me regretted burdening someone else with my secret but the other part of me, the sick part, regretted telling him because now I knew it would be twice as difficult to get away with drinking. Someone would be there to keep an eye on it, to sniff out the alcohol on my breath and to check my shopping bags. Chris joined me in the living room and sat opposite me. I drank the coffee slowly, savouring every drop. The longer my mouth was occupied the longer we'd have to stay silent and that's all I wanted for the time being. Chris knew everything now and he would try to help me. The day was awkward and unnecessary and as I couldn't sneak out for a drink we spoke. I allowed myself to be drawn into his concern, he googled alcoholism tests and asked me all the relevant questions. "Do you hide alcohol in the house?" He read.

I lied, "of course not." Immediately my mind jumped to every nook and cranny that had a bottle hidden in it. Underneath the bed there was a small cocktail bottle taped between the slats, behind the mirror in the hallway was a flat hip flask and the sofa had a hole in its base that concealed a fresh glass bottle that was unopened.

"How often do you drink?" He continued, reeling off the multiple choices. I chose the smaller of the three. He suspected nothing even though I could name 6 times in the last week that I had been drinking.

We sat in the silent living room knocking the questions back and forth.

"Can you drink more now than you could when you first started to drink?" he repeated, a simple yes or no question. I traced back to the first time.

It was a mild summer evening, about 8 years ago, and Anna and I had planned a sleepover, the normal tradition for the weekend of a 12-year-old. The decaying brick shed that lay in the corner of her garden was silent and secure. I'm not sure how we came to the decision to try alcohol for the first time but it had happened. I sat on the moth-eaten sofa and sank into the springs before she pulled out a single can of lager and a small bottle of cherry she had undoubtedly liberated from her grandparents. I pulled another two cans of larger from my own bag that my Dad would never miss. The sounds of the cans piercing their own seals echoed slightly in the empty structure, fizzing up and bubbling over. I instinctively doubled over and placed my mouth over the seal, I'd tasted beer before but never like this. This time, it was for a purpose. As a child, I'd watch my dad knock back three or four an evening without giving it a second thought. I hadn't given it a second thought, it was just something grownups drank and it wasn't something to shy away from. I took my first sip and the bitter taste hit the back of my throat. I coughed and spluttered and uttered the words "I'm a man." It was a joke and Anna found it hilarious as did I. Shortly, afterwards the euphoria hit me and we began dancing to the Elliot Minor CD that our teenage angst begged for. I remember the night drawing to a close after just one more pre-mixed cocktail and her mother telling us to quieten down.

I then thought to the previous night and how after a bottle of Gin I had managed to go to work and finish my day. The answer was yes, as it had always been.

"I'm not sure, probably not much more," I replied.

"Why do you drink?" he spoke, his words soft and understanding. This was a tough question. There was no multiple choice, a part of me thought that it was his idea and not the online test. It probably was. I thought carefully, silently deliberating my answer.

"I don't know!" I said finally. The answer wasn't completely a lie it just wasn't completely true. No, I didn't know why I drank, I had no idea why I decided to confess to him last night and I certainly had no idea why, at that moment, I felt like going to the shop and buying a bottle of vodka and sleeping until next week. Of course, he didn't believe me, to him there was a reason I wasn't revealing to him. Of course, there were reasons I drank but there are things in everyone's days that they can't handle. Everyone feels the need for an escape once in a while, I wasn't unique.

# Chapter 6
## *Track 6 – Beth Orton*
## *– Stolen Car*

Masturbation is one of life's gifts; we would not have been born with pleasurable genitalia and hands to use them if that wasn't their purpose. Think about it, tom-cats have barbs on their parts that allow for no pleasure and we live with clitorises and orgasms. It's hardly fair but none of us are complaining. There's something about sitting alone and wanking yourself to climax that makes every insufferable day just that bit more bearable. If you say you don't jack-off then you're lying. Everyone does it; no one talks about it.

It's part of the human condition that we all forget about and I find fascinating. You're sad? Masturbate. You're angry? Masturbate. Those few seconds of climax make everything seem clear. For a few seconds (if you're a woman, possibly a minute) everything is clear and you have the answers to every question you might have about the day, even if the only answer is something menial and irrelevant. Beforehand, you might be thinking about the stresses of work or how you're going to cope with the day but afterwards all you feel is clarity and peace that is unmatched by any meditation.

As I lay in my bed with a pool of rapidly cooling semen on my stomach I thought about the day, about how I would cope. Today was the beginning of my sobriety. I woke up and felt refreshed, I had no hangover and my phone had stayed silent. Everything was still a secret to those who were necessary. Chris had already left for work and as I lay in bed barely covered, I thought of all the possibilities. A few years work is not undone in a few days and I had no doubt about that. I knew it was going to take time, but did everyone else? In that clarity, I began to question my decision to become sober, now there was an expectation attached to everyone I knew that I had told and everyone I hadn't told would be kept watch by those I had.

As if nothing had happened, I got up for work. I would take today as I would take any other. I would join the swarm on the underground and board the train as always. As far as I was concerned, nothing had happened.

My day went as normal, Alex made his advances and I had declined. He questioned me all day asking if I was 'OK'. Being sober now had become odd to those who hadn't seen me otherwise. I was trying. My day couldn't end quickly enough and once it did, I left the shop as fast as my legs could carry, on to the train and onwards me home.

"You should let me sit," a quiet voice said from behind; my headphones were on and I turned to see a woman in her forties amongst the crowded train.

"Based on what assumption?" I removed one ear bud.

"Well?" She said matter of fact; clearly gesturing to the fact that she was a woman. I surveyed the train car, all the seats were taken and the isles were filling up business men and the like "I'm sorry but…" I replied. She quickly turned her nose in disgust, looking for support from the multiple strangers around her. Quickly and without thought, as I often have, I began my counter argument "Feminism is a two-way street; there are multiple people in their seats, none of them have offered them to you, why me? Why not that man?" I gestured to the man in his early twenties opposite me.

"Well you're younger," she began.

"And by that logic, I assume my job doesn't count either? I was up this morning the same as you and spent the last nine hours on my feet in a job I hate so people like you can buy things you don't need." She stayed silent as others began to look on to the conflict that was unfolding.

"As a woman, I'm sure you're used to waiting for lengthy periods of time for something to finish so you can leave even though it seems like you've been stuck for eternity, regardless of how tired you are; so you can sympathise and let me take a short break from my pathetic existence for a few minutes ok?" I finished. She said nothing else for the rest of the journey.

When I got home, Chris was already in his office. I looked to the hollowed sofa and my mind jumped to the hip flask behind the mirror. I wasn't actively thinking about getting drunk, I just knew in my mind that it was there and it had become a reflex almost to reach for the drink where I could. How long had I survived and continued to drink without anyone knowing? As I sat and listened to the movement above, I wasn't even sure if he'd heard me come in. Maybe he hadn't? I dropped my bag by the door as I always did, slowly moving towards the sofa. My hand reached under the gap between the chair and the floor and felt for the hole in the fabric. My fingers poked through the small gap, working their way through the stuffing in the seat until I felt the glass. I pulled at it, dragging it outward. I heard the sound of footsteps rapidly make their way down the stairs immediately pushing the bottle back and pulling my phone out of my pocket, remaining on the floor.

"What are you doing?" Chris asked, standing on the bottom step. I jolted and pretended not to notice him, standing up with my phone in my hand.

"I dropped my phone!" I smiled and quickly moved forward. I hugged him and we kissed.

Without hesitating he asked "Have you been drinking?" I was offended. Even if the truth was that I had I would still be offended.

"No," I quickly retorted. The problem was that if I acted offended, it looked like I had something to hide, if I acted too casual it would look like I was drunk. I had painted myself into a corner yet again. I pulled away slightly, without saying another word I smiled and moved up the stairs. Chris trailed behind me asking about my day as he always did and we spoke like normal as he followed me into the bedroom. I started unbuttoning my shirt as he continued to talk, telling me about his work that I didn't understand whilst I pretended to be interested. As I sat on the bed, he stood in the doorway and I nodded; smiling appropriately and answering where possible.

"Anyway," he finished, "I'll let you get dressed, I'm thinking Chinese tonight?" he smiled.

"Sounds perfect!" I replied sincerely, as he left the room, shutting the door behind him. I remained in my seat as my hand reached beneath the bed frame. I felt for the bottle taped between the slats until my fingers felt it. Pulling it out, my ears remained alert for his return. I finished the small cocktail bottle and put it in my underwear. As I sat on the bed, I let the wave of euphoria hit me; I lay back on the sheets and stared at the ceiling for a few minutes. My body suddenly jolted forward, I had to get dressed and act normal. This was going to be my life from now on, it was going to be a constant stream of hidden bottles and accusations. To every person that found out about my problem, I was another hazard, I would constantly be put under the spotlight. Every friend that slowly found out would begin to question every memorable evening we'd had and ask if it was because of the drink. I would ask myself the same things all the time, eventually you stop becoming so sure about everything around you and your world is filled with doubts. As I got dressed, these thoughts circled around my brain and even though the alcohol began to seep into me I knew that it couldn't go on.

"That's it," I said to myself "no more." As I had declared to myself earlier that day, the difference being this time was I meant it. I joined Chris in the living room shortly after where I was greeted with a hug. I had never felt an embrace as tight as the one he had me in at that moment. I stood silent, wondering for a moment.

"What's this in aid of?" I laughed, still standing in each other's arms,

"I just want to make you feel loved," he sincerely replied, moving his head to kiss me on the cheek. I said nothing.

In my head, we were people that had just met, lying on my single bed in my mother's house. The two of us had only known each other a few months and were quickly falling in love, or so we thought. We would lay there in the tiny boxed room for hours watching TV or playing video games or just talking nonsense to each other. We had just been on a weekend away and were officially a couple, still bright eyed and full of excitement for each other. He had just taken me to get a haircut, something more grown up, I had just cooked my first of many meals for him. A few beers or so were shared and he told me his love of red wine and as I poured out a glass, choosing a film cross legged on my bedroom floor he smiled. I caught his gaze, handing him his glass.

"What is it?" I grinned, turning my head, he joined me on the floor.

"I want to keep you forever," he said softly.

"Forever is a long time, you'll get sick of me," I took a sip.

"I'm already sick of you, I still want to keep you forever," he smiled again and kissed me gently.

I was back in our house with him, three years later. Forever didn't seem so long after all. How long could I keep this up? How long would it be until forever was over?

When people you know try to deter you from drinking, they all bring up stories about how someone they used to know, usually a person with so many prospects who was good looking, is now an alcoholic. They usually mention how they bumped into them in a garage or an off-licence buying a bottle of booze and how they're not so good looking anymore and the stories are usually told with disgust. There is never an air of sympathy towards the people who they used to call friends. When people talk about alcoholism in schools, they always show you the same pictures of the down and outs covered in their own piss and vomit; "don't be this guy" they'd say. Walking down a street seeing the men and women all red-faced and puffy eyed is meant to make us aware of the lowest points you can reach. But what nobody tells you, what they all fail to mention, is the side effects and withdrawals that these people are actually going through. They'll mention the degenerates parents and how it makes them feel, how they no longer have any friends and that they obviously didn't care enough. They'll ask you or themselves what they did to deserve being treated in that way, not what the alcoholics themselves are feeling.

There's no compassion towards them, to me, because 'they did this to themselves'. they chose to sit on the stoop outside Tesco with a can of white lightning at 11 a.m. on a Wednesday. But that's not all; according to modern education and social stigmas, they also chose to wake up and have their bodies convulse uncontrollably, providing they sleep at all. If they manage to get to sleep eventually, the sweats begin like a broken faucet that'll continue through three shirts and the thickest of bedsheets. After waking up cold and wet, they'll try to stand only to find that they have no feeling in their limbs as their whole body continues to shake, feebly hobbling towards whatever day they have planned. That's just the beginning, then there's the headaches, the unshakeable sick feeling, stomach cramps and in extreme cases hallucinations that make you question everything around you. That's what happens when they don't drink; waking up like this and knowing that it can stop or be made easier by just one drink, one tiny splash of alcohol can make things seem normal again. But they choose to do it right? They chose to live this way.

It's never as personal as people make it, the friends and parents of these people, providing they had them, were never intentionally the victims of these people's actions. It's more of an occupational hazard that comes with the territory.

Everyone has experienced this at least once in their lives, waking up in the morning bleary eyed with a head full of rocks and throat full of sand. Step one to getting sober would be getting over a mother of all hangovers. For some it's enough to put them off of drinking for a lifetime, for those of us who can't stop, it's merely a pause button on reality. Every hangover is just a temporary repercussion that can be solved by another drink. A sausage, an egg McMuffin and an iron Brü just wasn't going to cut it. As I awoke for work that day, I couldn't help but feel the impulse to call in sick. After all that's what this was, I was recovering from a sickness.

Throughout the day, I dealt with the unshakeable sick feeling in my stomach, like it was being scratched at from the inside, itching away at my digestive system. Sleeping that night would be no trouble at all, if I managed to survive the day the minute the sun set, I'd be straight to sleep. I was awoken at regular intervals in the night, cold and sweating only realising I didn't need to be awake for another few hours when I looked at the clock. It's a question to ask yourself, have you ever drank and lied to a partner about the volume? Have you ever drank to the point where you feel ill the next morning and can't remember the night before? When you drink, are you really responsible for your actions? If your answer is no then the real question is; do you have a problem?

Firstly, let me set the record straight, I have a problem. I'm not going to go into too much detail but you'll probably make an educated guess by the end of this story. I've always had a problem and whoever reads this that knows me, knows that it's true, also if you're reading this and you do know me, thanks. I thank you for always making it this far. Let me start by saying that not all withdrawal symptoms are the same as is the same with the substances you can get addicted to. For example, quitting your habit of five coffees a day won't make you itch nearly as much as ditching five cigarettes a day. Putting a drink down won't be as hard as pulling a needle away, but that doesn't change the fact that they are real and it is something the people you love will go through if they are, trying to break the habit. As I've mentioned before, it's not the same for everyone and even if you've done it, you may have had a different experience, even so, here's how I've seen it. (Pre warning: this is going to be a long one, so take a deep breath and thank me later.)

## Tremors, Nausea and Headache

Having a headache or feeling sick in the modern world is a fairly treatable ailment; pop a few paracetamols, drink some water and you're good to go. Wrong. A headache of this magnitude that makes you so dizzy that you see stars every time you close your eyes won't simply go away with a couple of painkillers and a pint of water (not water at least). Imagine you're walking down a street and out of nowhere, the Hulk punches you in between the eyes, you're blind, disoriented and all you can feel is the enormous pressure building between your ears. No amount of aspirin is going to heal that. Next, your stomach not only feels unsettled, it actually kind of burns. A dull burn, but a burning nonetheless, like putting out a candle with your bare fingers. It hardly stings for a second but after a few hours you want to rip your own insides out, this is all well and good if this is the only day you have to deal with it, of course. However, feeling it so intensely that you can't sleep, a different story. Finally, there are the tremors, the casual shaking of the hands that everyone notices and you can bet everyone will comment on. You blame it on low blood sugar and excuse yourself for a Lucozade and pretend it didn't happen. Then you try to sit at a dinner table or write something down and it's increasingly obvious that it is completely out of your control. Imagine eating a bowl of soup in an earthquake, nothing massive, maybe only a four on the Richter scale but still a difficult thing to explain.

## Sweating, Vomiting and Irritability

Sweating is never a nice experience, but when even a cold shower or sitting in a fridge can't quell the pools beneath your pits, let's just say that it's not pretty. It's also something that people definitely notice; If they're polite they won't mention it, if not, not only will you be visibly wet, you'll be visibly pissed. Which brings us to irritability, a calmer cousin to blind rage. Have you ever been annoyed with the way someone breathes? It's like that except you're shaking and sweating and every single person around you is snoring like a rhino. Eventually, you snap and everyone just thinks you're being a dick when actually you're sick and in pain and on top of that embarrassed having to come up with excuses for it constantly. If you're unlucky, you'll also have to excuse yourself every time something enters your stomach (yes even water) because your stomach simply cannot handle any more pressure. Vomiting can last for hours, it can last for days, it really depends how far you followed Alice down that rabbit hole.

## Fever, Seizures and Tactile Hallucinations

Now, let me preface this by saying that the next few are only for those completely committed to their trip to wonderland but nonetheless. So on top of the sweating, vomiting and being generally pissed off with the world, now your head's on fire and you're feeling things that don't exist. Having an itch you can't scratch is one of life's most irritating feelings but imagine having an itch you *literally* can't scratch because it simply doesn't exist. It almost feels like the itch is beneath your skin and the only way to get at it is to keep scratching until you reach it. You can scratch until your skin is raw but until you reach it, you'll never stop and to make it worse you're also burning. Remember, I said that your stomach was like a stubbed match? Well this fever is a house fire that match started. The heat just keeps being turned up like you're an inside-out oven and no amount of cold flannels to the forehead is going to help. It's a completely contradictory feeling, the sweats are cold but the head is the temperature of the sun. It's that hot, in fact, that it literally fries your brain, causing your entire body to tense up, writhing on the floor with your teeth clenched so hard that not even your own tongue is going to stop it. You may not remember it but it can be a truly terrifying experience to literally lose control of your limbs and almost chew your own tongue off.

## Nightmares and Insomnia

Lastly, if you've survived all of the above without a relapse, you're going to experience the worst insomnia of your life. In fact, that is the only reason this story exists. The insomnia has to be one of the most Ironic of the withdrawals because all you'll do is stay awake and dream of a medicated sleep. Usually, this is because it's been a lifetime since you fell asleep naturally, in fact, this is one of the things you'll think about as you're awake for nineteen hours. This is dangerous territory because the reality of thinking that you could sleep if you just went down that rabbit hole again, just a for a minute, you'd be able to rest. The problem therein lies that there is no such thing as 'just for a minute'. Alice didn't stop at the tea party, she carried on until she broke through the other side and even then, she went back a few years later only to the same thing. When you finally do sleep, the dreams you have will be so realistic that you'll wake up in a hot sweat upright like they do in the movies. They're not always nightmares but they are realistic, so realistic that I can honestly say I have woken up and had to ask myself if things really happened or not. The lines blur between wonderland and reality just as easily as before.

I'm not saying I speak for everyone and I know that everyone has a different experience, but I can only describe what I've been through. There are other types of withdrawal and I imagine some of them are much harder, the point is if you're reading this, you defeated your own Red Queen and travelled back through the looking-glass and all that jazz. It's not impossible to break the habit, sometimes you need some help but ultimately Alice got herself out of wonderland and so will you. If only I could give myself the wonderful advice, I've given to everyone else and truly listen to it. Truly give it the time and thought that I needed as and when I needed it. I speak frequently and openly about how I've dealt with things, how I've given my day to day life or living experience to this one identifier, but that's not the only thing I have.

# Chapter 7
## Track 7 – The Thorns
## – Among the Living

"Now I am quietly waiting for the catastrophe of my personality to seem beautiful again, and interesting, and modern."

Frank O'Hara, Meditations in an Emergency.

Everyone faces difficult situations in life. We all find ourselves in difficult situations at times. This is because, whoever we are and whatever we're doing, life is challenging. And we can't always predict what's going to happen. These situations, in turn, affect how we think and feel and when we're struggling with a tricky situation, it's easy to start thinking about things in negative ways. This then makes us feel upset, gives us an overwhelming sense of guilt. Your body tenses up, a heavy, sinking feeling sits within your chest and the idea that we may not be able to overcome whatever it is becomes so overwhelming that it often leads you into trouble. Especially, when lapsing is a coping method you're all too familiar with.

It's easy to put ourselves at risk by making 'seemingly irrelevant decisions' whatever stage of our recovery journey we're at, staying on track can be hard because we're likely to face temptations and adversity along the way. Unless we stay aware of the places and situations that are dangerous for us, we can set ourselves up to fail all too easy by making the previously mentioned 'seemingly irrelevant decisions'. By making choices that on the surface seem harmless, you can fool yourself into believing that it's not a lapse, it's not an issue and everything is still absolutely fine. "I'll just have one drink.", "I'll just text that ex that I miss them.", "I'll just look for reasons to hate myself because it's easier than trying to understand and come to terms with what is actually happening," and well, you get the idea. The truth is by doing this, you are actually (and often unknowingly) setting yourself on a path towards a high-risk situation. And the cycle continues.

Our risky choices may be deliberate or we may be unaware of them, we might even be blissfully unaware that everyone around us knows what might be a better decision to make but the urge to resist is so easy to give in to that by the time you've made the choice, it's too late. You get yourself into trouble because you're not thinking clearly about the choices you're making and you don't appreciate where your 'seemingly irrelevant decisions' are leading you. Like arranging to meet a friend on payday outside a pub or club or deliberately surrounding yourself with enablers because it's that much easier. Sometimes it's deliberate, sometimes it's purely coincidental, either way, we put ourselves in danger unnecessarily.

The difficulty lies in the ability to plan ahead and think about the choices you make, which is easier said than done. If you can anticipate high risk situations and recognise when you may be starting to work your way towards them, you can stop yourself from going any further. This ability is a learned skill and it comes with time, it's a strength that doesn't come naturally but it is one that's necessary. The part of the brain that pushes you to do these things and make these choices tends to put a bottle towards the part that knows it's wrong. The time it takes to learn is irrelevant, the point is that it's being learned and it's making those steps that counts for more than any amount of lapses you can count. The key, the honest truth, is learning to not be so hard on yourself and to realise that these things do, in fact, take time. You don't have to learn this skill alone and those who are willing to help teach you, will be there until you can do it alone and when that day comes, the amount of strength you will have gained will never leave you, allowing everything else to fall into place.

A few weeks had passed since what I would later refer to only as 'the incident'. The more time went by, the less I thought about it and the less it would be real. Like a nightmare you had re-occur as a child that the more you pushed it away, it was as if the demon never existed in the first place. I hadn't spoken about it and my thirst had quelled. For the first time in what felt like forever, I could finally breathe. Like the city would breathe new life everyday with the changing winds, I too was finally breathing. The thirst had subsided but I knew as I was beginning to breathe, all it would take was another gust of wind to knock me back down. I would walk down the street and suddenly be reminded of his breath or the smell of alcohol and stale cigarettes. The sensation would be so intense that my whole body would ache and all of a sudden, I'd find myself glancing at a corner shop toying with the idea of going inside. Sometimes I'd even go in, I'd get up to the counter, a bottle of blue Fanta from the fridge laid out on the counter. My eyes would glance over the clerks shoulders, could I get away with this? Could I justify just one bottle, one tiny drink, after all, it has been so long that I'd earned it. I could even call it a celebration of sobriety and let it slip this once. I'd usually just wimp out and slam a pound coin on the counter and leave before I could tempt myself.

Days turned to weeks and weeks turned to months. Nothing had changed. Just yet anyway. I found that routine was the key for success, wake up, coffee, go to work, eat breakfast and so on. Walk the same route every day, avoiding all the obstacles; including true temptation. Take that previously mentioned map and turn it upside down, even if it meant taking longer than normal just to keep focused. The monotony of routine sometimes felt like a rope that was pulling me closer towards boredom and ultimately the lapse in both judgement and character but at the same time, it was keeping me tethered. The same thing day after day meant that I couldn't be caught off guard and that I could prepare myself to avoid the risky nature of my behaviour, or so I thought. A day like any other, it started off as normal. I opened my eyes to the sound of birds and the annoyingly obnoxious alarm that

I usually did. The back of Chris's head was the first thing my blurred vision could make out. I reached out a quivering arm and pulled him in, disturbing his sleep slightly and as he turned his head, his eyes opened accompanied with a smile directed at me.

"Morning!" he whispered, kissing me gently as I returned the sentiment. Sitting up, I let out a yawn and a sigh, reaching over to silence the alarm. I am here, this is now and I am a part of the world again. I crawled to the door, asking the everyday "Tea?", it was too early for full sentences, I decided. He smiled and nodded before rolling over and closing his eyes. I knew he wouldn't be awake when I returned. As I stepped into the hallway and on to the bathroom, the sound of rain lightly kissed the windows and I felt the sudden annoyance that I had to leave the comfort of the here and now and be thrust into *then.* Then, where the world was wet and cold and I would be forced back into the clockwork beehive as miserable as always. As I shifted towards the toilet, I let out an audible sigh, locking eyes on the toilet. Immediately, I was made to think about my regular hiding spot. I knew there would be nothing there, there hadn't been for some time and yet I instinctively craned my neck behind the back, *"just to be sure"* I thought to myself. I was correct. I went about my business, flushed and moved to the kitchen. I'd be lying If I didn't feel some kind of resentment or annoyance that I was right. *"No, this is the right choice"* I whispered. Everything went back to focus on the routine, the mundane few moments of a morning that shared no significance. Moments that when re-telling the story of your day wouldn't even be a second thought. Eat breakfast, get dressed, drink coffee; the same as it was every day. Even with the everyday routine, however, there were moments that would catch me off guard. The rope would be tugged one way or the other and I'd recall those later on. The way Chris smiled before I left or the way he'd sleep so peacefully half covered and probably cold. When I'd leave the flat, the look of a child being dragged to school that would make me stop and think, me too kid, *me too.* I arrived at work in the normal timely manner I would every shift day; I was alone today. A day that I could rest and not have to fight off any unwanted advances. A day that I would have to keep my mind distracted on my own. That was a scary thought. The endeavour of just simply being human. What did that mean?

There are people who find things beautiful within you and will nurture them and encourage the most destructive parts of you until it's too much. Perhaps, you have a sharp tongue and people applaud your honesty, maybe you'll never say no to a night out and people will use this to their advantage and maybe you have a short temper and people will see this as a reason to keep you as a kind of friend-body guard. Amongst other personality traits (too numerous to list) that all seem great in the beginning, wear thin eventually. This then leaves you with no choice but to simply wait.

What does it mean to be a good person? Is it the ability to do good things or notice when something's wrong and step in? Is it knowing when the classic idea of the 'right thing' may not necessarily be the right thing to do for that situation?

Can you be defined as a good person if you don't know right from wrong? The idea that there is such a thing as good and bad in people is that we have a sense of this. For example, a shark isn't considered evil because we perceive that it doesn't have a moral compass, it eats and swims without feeling guilty for keeping itself alive. The bee stings out of instinct and doesn't consider the fact that it'll die after therefore suggesting it's not making a conscious choice to do the right thing and not harm living things. I believe, Morality stems from knowing what's right and wrong and choosing thereafter however where is the line?

Can a good person still do bad things and vice versa? Giving to the homeless, charities, being kind and generous, eating healthy and exercising, maybe even going as far as being vegetarian. Listening to others and giving time to people around you, speaking in turn and being honest and doing everything you can to not hurt another person—all things universally considered good. Murder, violence, taking drugs or stealing. Lying, speeding, texting while driving and interrupting people. Stomping your feet and eating boiled eggs on a train, chewing with your mouth open, swearing and ignorance or being rude and loud in public—all things universally considered bad. Yes, there is a sliding scale, but can someone do a bad thing in order to be good? Can you steal food to feed a homeless person? Can you lie to do everything you can to not hurt someone? Can you do all of this and be considered simply as good, or bad?

In terms of a self-proclaimed bad deed, recognising it's bad is half the battle. In my experience, it no longer becomes about if you can be drunk enough, the question is can you be sober enough? Attempting to cancel out the bad with good to prevent more waiting. In order to stop from having to repeat the philosophy of Frank O'hara and have to wait for your catastrophic personality to be beautiful again; can you be sober enough that all your jokes are still funny and your words aren't slurred? Can you still be sober enough that you can still hold a conversation and be honest with everyone you meet?

Can you still be sober enough to get a day's work done and go out with friends and not have anyone question what you do? Can you be honest enough? Can you be honest with yourself to the point where you know that you're lying?

Can you realise when you've done wrong and that your choices have led you down the wrong path and can you even make the right choices after that fact? Can you be good enough? As these thoughts strolled through my mind like a new mother does in the park with a pram, that's when I felt it. the gentle and subtle vibration of my phone in my pocket. As far as work goes, it was a particularly quiet day and I had put it down to the weather but as I reached down to see who or what was causing the vibration, I had a sudden thought that there was something more than I had first thought. It was an unfamiliar number that appeared on my text screen. Had I deleted this number previously or was it an accident? Maybe it wasn't meant for me. My heart skipped a beat, was it John trying to contact me again? I hadn't heard from him since 'the incident', for all I knew, his body had started to rot where I'd left him. I didn't care, as far as anyone was concerned, I was never there, we didn't know each other. Upon reading through, I *did* recognise the anonymous messenger, I had simply chosen not to save it in the first place. I sighed with relief and read on. It was Chris' old stepfather. What did he want with me? It was a generic small-talk text, "Hi, how are you, hope you're keeping well"—that sort of thing. It was innocent, it didn't mean anything, but for now, I would quietly wait for it to implode. As he continued to talk, I noticed the more sinister undertones of his conversation. He would reference my sexuality like an open book, told me I was a good-looking lad and that Chris and I were a good-looking couple. I didn't tell Chris immediately, instead I ignored it, for now. As I stood in silence thinking of all the possible reasons he could have for wanting to talk to me, I looked back to six months ago, when we were first introduced.

# Chapter 8
## *Track 8 – Ella Vos*
## *– Lonely Road*

I was sat at a family birthday party. It was a happy occasion, something we all needed. Chris wasn't there because of some prior work commitment, however everyone would ask, "where is he? what is he doing?" It's like we no longer become James of XYZ. We are the partners we choose. That's the message we get, from day one, the second that we find someone we like or even think we love, we're measured against that, to the point where it's so easy to lose yourself. It was springtime and earlier that day we had been to the flat to move all the furniture in, ready to unpack when he returned from work. More small talk followed;

"Are you excited?"

"Are you Nervous?"

"You've already moved jobs that's good!" everything one would expect.

As I was drinking an unusually strong cocktail made from some form of Gin that my aunt had thrown together, picking at the generic spread of buffet sausage rolls and quiche, I felt my phone vibrate in the pocket of my skinny jeans. I never had the ringer on, there's something slightly obnoxious and even daunting about announcing to everyone in a room via ring-tone that someone is contacting you. I answered my phone, took myself out of the room because when I heard the silence of him, I knew something was wrong. I had a drink (or five) at this point because the people I was surrounded by had no idea the extent of the issue that had occurred. His voice was steady, calm and un-telling. I slurred "What's wrong?"

"Nothing, I just needed to hear your voice."

After two years together, I knew this was a lie. There was something wrong. I prodded.

"My brother has just died," he spoke, he said his name so easily that it didn't seem real. I had spoken with him, I considered us friendly but nothing can compare with the loss of someone so close to you that the thought of being without them makes you tense up every time. I couldn't Imagine what was going through his mind at this point so I calmly and with every amount of tact and sincerity, I replied simply "What happened?"

"They're not sure, I'm heading to my Dad's now…" he said blankly, he's voice trailed off and I could hear the traffic in the background, my voice was lost in the party that was happening behind me. Gin in hand I took another drink, finishing the potent cocktail. There was a moment of silence.

"Do you want me to be there?" I stupidly asked, trying not to pry. I didn't want to be invasive because we'd never spent much time in that circle, however, to follow my sincerity, I knew I had to do something. As I offered a slightly drunk, aunty refilled my glass making me move to the front garden so I could hear. I continued to drink.

"Yes," he replied, his voice quivering slightly, trying to hide the true emotion. I was a town over and knew it was unlikely to be able to travel at that time of night in the middle of a birthday party with a legal driver or an affordable taxi. Something inside of me that moment forgot about the logic and I was washed with a sudden sense of duty. When someone you love is in pain or needs support, there is no logic. You work out the practical cost of an hour-long taxi ride, you work out the logistics of finding an address in a different county and you just forget all sense of base logic. Nothing seems like too much of a hassle. I gained all the information I needed, told him I loved him and that I'd be there soon. The logistics were a work in progress.

Still holding my cocktail, I raced inside, wading through the crowd to find my mother, if we were at home, I could've navigated a taxi or even a bus to get me close but this time, I was completely reliant on the sober few with a car. I had an hour drive to navigate being inebriated by three cocktails that could have legally been a science experiment. I went through the room, asking them if they could drive and begging for a ride, all the while texting Chris of his status (physical and emotional) the latter gaining more clarity than the other. As the tide of clarity rolled in so did the alcohol and as I searched for anyone that could even drive, I was handed another cocktail, the taste of brandy and gin colliding to create a fog that settled on my mind. I ran into my cousin and brother who jumped at the chance to drive me. Finally, texting Chris, I was leaving and that it'd be an hour, I made my way to a hub of grief, drunk and probably useless. When I arrived, we spoke for a few minutes joined by his family, drinking tea and letting them discuss and reminisce about times I knew nothing about. As it hit midnight, I was shown to the room we would be staying in, "I'll join you in a second," Chris said, retreating back to his family. He was always private and I listened to his footsteps, they stopped half way down the stairs, static. He was crying, although he would never admit it or let it show. He joined me a few minutes later and I pretended not to notice. We were alone and preparing to sleep, he let go for a few seconds and fell into my arms, sobbing gently. I stayed in silence. He kissed me and behind that one kiss I could feel everything he was feeling. In that moment, I knew that there was confusion and anger and love all thrown together with no rhyme or reason to justify it. We moved to the bed and that night he laid upon my chest in silence until the morning came and we were forced to face another day.

The next few weeks passed and Chris had returned to work and I had moved into our new life alone. I had started work and was building a relationship with Alex as was expected. A perfectly smooth transition or so I thought. The day of the funeral came and I travelled back to be with Chris. The day of any funeral, no matter who's, is never a pleasant one. The morning was like any other, make the tea, make the toast make sure everyone is catered for as we fill a room with black suits and dresses. I stayed out of the way glued to the kettle and kitchen sink ensuring everyone was taken care of because it wasn't my funeral to attend. The service was beautiful and as we sat in the church, I turned to Chris, his face was blank and he was almost smiling. I knew that everything was dealt with behind closed doors though, I had never seen him really cry apart from that. As we stood over the grave, the coffin slowly being lowered in, I stared into the soil. I noticed the polish of the wood and how beautiful the surrounding grounds were and suddenly, I was reminded that there was someone's life in that wooden box. Someone's son, father, boyfriend or work colleague, every first step or kiss or every time he held the door for a stranger, all of that was now encased in a wooden box that was slowly lowered into the ground. I was hypnotised by that thought only broken from it when I felt Chris's hand pulling me towards the car. The journey to the wake was silent.

First impressions are always important, they say it takes three to five seconds upon meeting someone for the first time for you to make a snap judgement. Is this person likeable? Are they funny? Are they annoying? All of this is decided subconsciously within just a few short seconds. In that first handshake and hello we've decided whether or not a conversation can continue. Some of us are better at making first impressions than others and it takes a while for the person to really show their true colours, like a long con with only one end goal, to befriend someone and gain their trust. Other people are more honest, they hide behind social graces or common politeness, what you see is what you get and those people are infinitely easier to navigate. Chris's old stepfather was not one of those people. He was an older gentleman who was only in Chris' life through his early adolescence, I've never known the full story of why him and Chris's mother divorced and quite frankly, I never asked, however knowing what I know now, it doesn't surprise me. As the car arrived at the pub where the wake was being held, I could see familiar faces, waiting outside and smoking. When people cry, it's as if they've removed a mask and their face changes so once you see that face, the face they hold on a day-to-day can sometimes be unrecognisable. Chris and I waded through the crowd of smoke and instantly were greeted by his old stepfather, hand extended pulling Chris in for a friendly hug.

"Hiya, I'm Andy, lovely to meet you James, heard so much about you!" he enthusiastically repeated his actions, pulling me in for an awkward hug and I just smiled awkwardly responding with nothing but a "You too." He immediately offered to buy us both a drink and without hesitation, I asked for whatever lager they had on tap. Andy was married with two kids, both of whom were nowhere to be seen and as the afternoon progressed, I had an overwhelming sense that he had more time invested in mine and Chris's relationship than we were. He probed with questions about our lives, what I did for a living, how we're finding our new home, general small talk. I got the impression he was the perfect example of a grown man chasing his youth trying to live through the youngest men he knows. the day drew on and after a few pints, Chris and I went outside. He placed a cigarette between his teeth and handed the pack to me. The click of his lighter drowned out in the din of multiple guests conversation, cupping his hands, he moved towards mine. We both inhaled, the ashy taste veiled in menthol filling my lungs. "He seems like a character!" I exhaled allowing the plume of smoke to surround us both.

"He is. We haven't spoken in years," exhaling his cigarette, moving forward to lean on a railing that encased the smoking area.

"Who's that?" I quizzed, he seemed to know a lot about recent events and the charisma Andy had made me think they kept in touch. I was never one to pry or question who Tom was texting or calling so for all I knew they could've been. He turned to me, flicking the butt of his cigarette onto the concrete, I shortly followed.

"We just lost contact!" he said blankly, as if there was more than he was letting on. I didn't pry and we re-joined the party. Without hesitation, Andy cornered us again, offering us both another pint of lager and we complied.

"Hey boys, we should keep in touch!" he exclaimed, pulling out his phone, leaving us no choice but to enter our numbers. Maybe he was just being friendly, maybe he was just lonely but whatever his intentions were, I gave him no mind. We left shortly after returning to the safety of Chris's father's house continuing the day as if nothing had changed. The following morning, we boarded a train back to our new flat and the new lives we had tried to start.

As we entered the dimly lit maisonette that evening, boxes of Chris things still stacked in various rooms, I moved to the kitchen and began making tea. Chris moved towards the living room and sat down. The kitchen had a small window connecting it to the living space so I could see as he dropped his bags and slumped onto the small blue sofa that his eyes were glassy and had a vacant look to them.

"I'm thinking we just order Chinese tonight?" I called through, trying to make eye contact. Silence. He continued to stare blankly into space. The kettle clicked as I turned to the various cabinets, pulling down mugs and sugar. I made the tea and made my way through to the living room, setting down his on the coffee table. He said nothing, his reflection in the dormant TV staring back at us. I grabbed the remote and the sound of Channel 4's "8 out of 10 Cats" faded in with Jimmy Carr's distinct laugh coming into focus. "We've had a few menus posted through, it doesn't have to be Chinese?" I feebly and unsuccessfully tried to make conversation, taking a seat in the armchair besides him.

"Whatever!" he replied. He was quiet and unengaged.

"What's up? Talk to me!" I placed my hand on his knee. In that moment his eyes filled with tears and the glassy expression broke. Suddenly he was back in the room and I shot up to sit beside him. In everything that had happened that day, it had finally dawned on him the gravity of the situation. I cradled him in my arms and we sat in silence as the TV continued on, unheard and uninteresting.

# Chapter 9
## *Track 9 – Jefferson Airplane*
## *– White Rabbit*

People lose things, they just do. It happens throughout the day and throughout our lives without question. Whether that be our phones or wallets or sense of self, on a daily basis, people lose things.

We've all felt our hearts drop when we reach for something in our pockets that isn't there; it's like walking up the stairs in the dark and assuming there's an extra step. As your foot falls so does your stomach, the feeling of loss becomes all too real. It's like crossing the street and not realising a car is speeding towards you, you stop in the headlights and you can feel your stomach somersault. When you lose it's the same feeling.

I'm speaking strictly material of course, but what happens when we lose something more personal? What do we do when we lose something that can't be replaced or something that doesn't sit in our pockets?

People lose things but they also lose people, they lose emotion or respect or even themselves. Waking up and realising you've lost yourself gives you the same sense of stomach dropping, heart stopping loss that reaching for the wallet in your pocket does. In the same way reaching for someone who isn't there any more does.

When the day arrives that you realise a person is no longer there, you experience the same sense of loss you would have and, in some ways, you wish it were as easy as losing a phone. There are many factors to losing a person; they can choose to go or they can be taken. You can push them away and cause them to become lost or you yourself can just become lost in everything you were once so sure of, causing other people to lose you. All of a sudden, your foot is falling through the dark again, you're crossing the street, your heart is pounding and you're left with the realisation that someone just isn't there. You've lost them, you've lost it and everything.

You reach out and they don't acknowledge you, you fall and they don't catch you like they used to and they definitely don't give you the time of day. Losing people is hard but in the same way that your foot falls and reaches ground or the car doesn't hit you, you'll feel that sense of relief, eventually.

When you lose yourself, your motivation or sense of being, it can be harder to consider the reasons why you're perhaps doing the things you are. Waking up becomes difficult and you wish that you hadn't because being asleep is easier. When you lose yourself, it isn't as easy as reaching the ground or asking someone to help you find it, no one knows where it's gone or where you last saw it, it's just gone. Before you know it, it's difficult to make breakfast or to listen to music or go to work because you've just lost that light that everyone talks about when they meet you.

In the same way that you find your phone after panicking or your feet finally find the ground, so can you. You can find yourself again in little things you do every day. You can find yourself in the spontaneous karaoke sessions with your best friend or find yourself in a family meal. You find yourself in everyone that smiles at you whether that be a cashier or a stranger on the street. You can find yourself in the good deeds you do every day or in the family you have around you but you are there. By all means lose yourself, but lose yourself in a song or a conversation that you're passionate about. Lose yourself in a musical or a film that you connect with and don't be afraid to feel it all. Lose yourself but be ready to pick yourself straight back up and continue on. That day in the shop, as I stared at the text message from an otherwise stranger, I began to lose something in myself.

The day dragged itself out with customers slowly trickling in throughout the day, hour by hour until it was finally time for me to leave. All the while, a conversation had been kept between Andy and I, each question and subject becoming more and more probing than the last. It was as if the part of my brain that continued to push me to respond, to react instead of ignore had put a glass to the part of that knew on some level that this was all wrong. I was no longer able to think clearly and as I left the shop for the day, closing the shutters behind me and entering the street, my feet automatically meandered into the local corner shop just a few minutes from the train station. It was still raining and as the bell from the shops door chimed a crack of thunder broke out, causing me to be bought back down to Earth and the reality I had forgotten about. I felt my phone in my pocket again, opening the lock screen to reveal another message. I still hadn't saved his number. "You boys up to anything tonight?" he asked.

"Nothing that I know of, the weather's awful," I replied, accompanied by a frowning emoji, naturally. I found myself at the counter, laying my phone in front of me as I watched the screen anticipating a quick response.

"Half a Smirnoff, please," I said, without hesitation flashing my I.D at the clerk, pulling my debit card from the wallet, ready to pay. I received a reply. Entering my card into the reader, followed by my pin number, I moved the bottle from the clerks hands to the inside pocket of my jacket.

"Ah, best, get yourself in the warmth and out of those clothes." His text read, followed by a winking face and the infamous aubergine emoji. As I left the shop, I replaced my phone in my pocket and could hear the sound of vodka knocking against the glass bottle that was close to my chest, moving with every step towards the station. The rain continued to pour, followed by another clap of thunder as my feet waded through the various puddles that had settled on the street. It had been weeks since I had even thought of a drink, the house was empty, Chris knew my secret and was trying to help me and yet before I could explain it or even begin to think about the repercussions, I had broken that stride. It didn't make sense because I hadn't tried to make sense of it and as I entered the station, I immediately ducked in to the public access toilets. Slipping into the nearest stall, locking the door behind me, I pulled my phone from my pocket and sat on the closed toilet. I stared at Andy's message for a moment, contemplating a reply, silently waiting for something to pull me back to reality and pull me back from the decisions I was making. Then I felt the vibration once more, this time from Chris. He had been out unusually late for work that day somewhere in central London and because of the weather delays were to be expected.

"Trains are all delayed, we're still not finished so I'm going to be super late, sorry!" followed by a frowning emoji, I pulled the vodka from my pocket. I could hear movement outside of the stall and I waited from the hand dryer to be activated so the sound of a glass bottle being opened would be silenced in the hollow, ceramic room.

"That's ok, I'll make dinner, just let me know when you're close and I'll heat it up," I replied, taking a large sip from the bottle. For weeks my throat had missed the faint sting of the spirit. It tasted sweet and bitter like I had been yearning for the warmth for weeks. I flushed the empty toilet so I could replace the top. I returned the bottle to the inside of my jacket and left for the platform. The rain had built up on the stairs as my train arrived and people began to rush. I walked at my normal pace and stepped into the first available carriage; the clockwork beehive was in a panic that they may not return to their homes in the expected time as Chris wouldn't.

As I approached my front door, dripping from the rain that hadn't subsided, I took another sip from the bottle. It was as if I was anticipating Chris being on the other side even though I knew it wasn't true. Like a last effort before having to act sober again. Turning the key and entering the empty and dark hallway I was greeted by expected silence as usual. My coat was heavy with water and my hair represented that of a drowned rat.

"Must invest in an umbrella!" I thought to myself, dropping my bag on the floor and hanging my coat by the door. I removed the bottle and moved to the kitchen, placing it on the counter. It was the menial tasks like this of the day to day routine that kept me grounded, so why were these the hardest? Cook dinner from whatever we had in the house, replace the wet clothes with dry ones, clean up after myself, eat, all of these things seemed like chores as opposed to something that should come naturally. It wasn't like breathing where it came naturally and more of a job that had to be earned. My reward, however, was the bottle once more.

Once again, I found myself surrounded by warm bath. As it started to turn cold, I looked up with a glassy eyed blank expression. My bathroom ceiling became a white washed reverie as I came crashing back to reality. The rain continued its gentle beat against my windows followed by another rumble of thunder. I moved my eyes towards the clear, squared bottle that rest upon my bathroom tiles. I was taken back to the beginning. As the bittersweet taste of vodka burned my throat again, I slipped back into the water and let it grow even colder. Another crash of thunder. Holding the bottle just above the water, I watched the ripples echo across my body before finishing it completely. It no longer burned and instead hugged me from the inside. I closed my eyes for a moment. My head span and I slipped beneath the surface as images of Chris began to play like an old film. Grainy and foggy, I was reminded of his smile, his gentle laugh. I saw him cry that night and I saw us falling into each other naked and unafraid. I saw Johns face as it loomed over me, the smell of smoke and his heavy breath, I saw the stock room shelves rattle and the train passing me by as the blue ghost fell on to the tracks. Thunder crashed from above and I was bought back. It was no longer grainy and I took a breath as I continued to sit in the water, the bottle lay floating slightly beside me. I pulled myself out and stood there for a moment with nothing but the gentle patter of the outside world. Before drying myself off, I immediately removed the bottle and let the water out, watching as it lowered and circled the drain. My body gently swayed as I turned to retrieve my towel and left the bathroom to change.

I kept the bottle in my hand the entire time as I moved from down the stairs dressed only in a cheap hoodie and old pyjama bottoms. I'd brushed my hair back out of my face, still dripping wet, as the living room remained silent and empty. Moving towards the kitchen I rested the bottle on the counter, retrieving the cigarettes that were hidden atop the cabinets, just where they were supposed to be. There were only two left, meaning Chris had been having a few 'emergencies' of his own, I didn't mind because unlike him, they were where they were supposed to be, I thought. As that thought seeped through the fog in my mind, I was instantly reminded that I still had no idea where he was. In fact, I hadn't checked my phone since I left the station. My coat remained hanging by the door and my phone remained inside one of the soggy pockets. I placed the cigarettes inside my hoodie and took the bottle from the side. I couldn't simply put the bottle in the bin, unless I was going to empty the bin after to clear away the evidence and at this point in the day anyone who knew me, knew that wasn't going to happen. The previous sense of guilt and weight that I had carried home was gradually lifting and filling the silence with something I hadn't had in a while, clarity. My brain had switched over to the person I was when this started, maybe I was still unhappy but with a bottle by my side, I didn't care. With the bottle in my hand, I could make clear choices that, even if only for a moment, would give me pleasure. The most carnal, instinctive kind of pleasure that no one could make sense of, but me. I looked into my phone's screen, faced with a darkened version of my own reflection and with the press of a button the screen had lit up. There it was, the unsaved number I had been half-heartedly avoiding for the past couple of hours with a few messages to follow but none from Chris.

As I unlocked the screen, I could see that it was already 9:00 p.m. so before I moved from the door, I sent a new message to Chris asking where he was. I had forgotten about Andy for the time being and as I listened out for anything, I moved to the balcony. The sliding glass doors opened with ease and the smell of rain filled the air yet the sound of the expected accompaniment was absent. The rain had finally subsided. Still barefoot, bottle and phone in hand, I stepped outside and the cold rainwater left me unaffected as the alcohol settled into safe tipsiness. I stared vacantly into the darkness beyond the edge of the balcony, my mouth had turned dry, reaching for a cigarette, I glanced at my phone and saw Andy's name again. My eyes shifted to the bottle that I still held in the other hand and I began to laugh, I was laughing at the ludicrous notion that some older man was trying to make conversation with me (a total stranger) and I was laughing at the fact that this had all happened before. I thought back to being underwater and the image of John's face replaying in my mind and before I could stop myself, I threw the bottle over the edge. In that moment, as the glass shattered against the pavement, through the mindless giggling that had taken over, I crouched down, pulling a cigarette from my pocket and simply whispered, "Fuck."

Once I had finished my cigarette, my phone still in hand, waves began to crash upon me. Waves of a drunken stupor that I hadn't felt in some time. My feet remained wet and cold but the vodka meant that I didn't care as I flung myself backwards onto the sofa, reaching for the remote and regaining focus. It was at this point that I had made the decision that work would have to wait, whatever the outcome of this evening, I would not be going to work in the morning. Truth be told, whether this was a drunken decision or not, I didn't want to face Alex. I knew I was slipping back into the bad habits I thought I had, maybe left behind after wearing them on my sleeve; facing him with the hangover I was inevitably going to give myself didn't seem like a good idea. Still no word from Chris, yet Andy had sent more messages. I took a deep sigh, grinning slightly, I opened the messages. As I scrolled through, each one became subtly more and more suggestive. It wasn't obvious at first, it was the odd comment about making sure I washed behind the ears in the bath, making sure I got out of the wet clothes and as they slowly progressed, the occasional internet meme pushed its way through, usually of the suggestive variety. I merely replied with "LOL" and nothing more. In my head, I knew that even one reply was encouragement enough for his kind. What exactly was 'his kind'? I hear you ask. Andy was the kind of man that had spent his entire life belittled by a conservative family that didn't understand anything that wasn't northern or traditional. As a result, he had spent years perfecting the art of manipulation, micro-managing every aspect of his life so that if things went wrong, he would either look like the hero or the victim. Probably he also had a very tiny penis. I had dealt with men like this previously and those were the only ground of my intrusive theory, that and the bottle of vodka I had just drank neat.

The conversation went dry. I could sense that he was pushing for something but I wasn't sure what. The TV droned on in the background, it was an old episode of 'Cats does countdown' and as the numbers round presented itself, I was immediately made to think of Chris; he was always competitive and was always able to beat me on occasion even the panel on the show. It was well past 10:00 p.m. at this point and still no word. Concerned, I reached for my phone once more, opening the messaging app. I immediately sent a message expressing my concern and asking where he was. With no one else to talk to, the vodka haze beginning to fade, I turned to Andy.

"Chris still not home, bored!" followed by a sleeping emoji. As I hit send, my body carried me to the front door. Without thinking I placed on an old pair of trainers, still dressed in an old hoodie and pyjama bottoms, I headed for the door. The shop below us didn't shut until midnight. As I pulled my coat on, I received a response, again not from Chris.

"Oh no, hope you're behaving," he virtually winked.

"I resent the accusation that I'd be doing otherwise," I bantered back. The shop was less than two minutes from our front door and they knew my face. As with most habits, not only are they hard to break, but they become part of routine. I didn't need my whole wallet, just whatever cash remained in the bottom of my coat pocket. Reaching inside the slightly damp pocket, I could hear the rustling of change against my keys. Balled up in my fist, I pulled the coins from inside, £5 in total. This wasn't enough for vodka, however two bottles of wine would be no problem. I picked up two white bottles and returned to the safety of my silent and unjudging flat.

We've all heard the old saying that "A drunk mind speaks a sober heart" and whilst that's a beautiful sentiment, I find that it's not entirely true. As I drank directly from the first bottle of wine, I continued to banter back and forth, bordering on flirting and had I not been polishing off a bottle of wine to myself, maybe I wouldn't have been so quick to spar that way, however, I held the consciousness of my actions. If it were a cartoon, a cricket would be on my shoulder and I would have brushed him off. I would have ignored every direction my moral compass was directing me, drunk or sober.

With that final thought, I checked my phone one last time. Still nothing. I finished the last of the bottle I held in my hand, leaving the other on the table. I grabbed a scrap of paper and drunkenly scrawled in black biro, "I thought you could use it, enjoy." I placed the bottle in the centre of the table and set a place as if Chris were about to walk in the door any second and placed his dinner at a seat leaving only a wine glass beside the plate.

As I crawled into bed, the taste of stale wine lingered on my breath and my eyes became heavy. My mind kept back-tracking to the men I had dealt with before, to name a few, I thought of John, of his charming smile and his ability to know what I wanted, even if it was bad for me. I thought of Chris and how he made me feel safe and secure yet lost all at the same time. I thought of Alex and his carnal and raw animal instinct that seemed to dissipate the minute it was over and I thought of how I liked that. As I continued to flick through the channels, my phone kept vibrating. I had opened the floodgates and I was willing to get lost.

# Chapter 10
## *Track 10 – Maggie Rogers*
## *– Falling Water*

Throughout history in many cultures across the world, in religions and myths, people have been consistently surrounded by the weight of one's soul or actions. In Ancient Egypt, some believed the final trial (and I'm watering this down) was to be presented with a balance that was used to weigh their heart against the feather of Maat. If the deceased's heart balanced with the feather of Maat, Thoth would record the result and they would be presented to Osiris, who admitted them into the 'heaven'. However, if their heart was heavier than the feather, it was to be devoured by the Goddess Ammit, essentially 'sending them to hell'. In short, in Greek mythology Zeus hung his scales equally balanced with both sides of life and death, where the fates of Achilles and Memnon were in the balance held by Hermes. The Bible even has Archangel Michael in charge of the 'last judgement' in which again, a soul is weighed. I could go on but you get the idea. For centuries we've been fixated on the idea of balance and keeping things in our favour.

There are so many aspects of our lives that are concerned with keeping things together or with some sort of positive reward when we're finally forced on to those scales, does the bad weigh on us more than the good? What side are our choices adding to? Moreover, are the people we surround ourselves with adding to the weight and once it's on there can we take it off? I suppose, that depends on your idea of fate or what's right and wrong. Being off-balance can look different to everyone, to the people who truly know us it should be obvious, however, if you've had the scales monitored for a long time, it's all too easy to forge the numbers. Either way, there's always a possibility to tip the scales, one way or the other and that's when I believe you can no longer take away from the bad. The scales will forever be off-balance.

Also, for centuries humanity has come up with ways to shield ourselves from (or at least help us) from what we would coin overindulging 'sins' if you like. People go to church, they pray, some people go to support groups like weight watchers or AA and in many ways, this makes us feel like the scales may actually be tipping in our favour. Maybe we can even take some of the weight off and restore some of the balance. When we're off-balance it's often easier to keep tipping, like leaning back in a chair at school. Two of the chair legs are in the air whilst the two on the back remain somewhat on the ground, at this point you're suspended, perhaps even holding on to the edge of a table. As you continue to lean your fingertips move closer and closer towards the edge of the only thing keeping you steady, you lose your grip and, in that moment,, your stomach flips upside down as you are sent straight to the ground, hitting it with such force it knocks the wind out of your lungs. Now that you're on the ground with everyone around you staring, are the people around you going to pull you backup and replace your chair? Are they going to push themselves back and join you on the ground? Or are they going to encourage you to stay down? We would all like to think the immediate answer is option number one but if you think about it, you could probably only say that's true for a small percentage of the people around you.

Alongside balance, we've always believed that misery loves company, which is why we will often find ourselves on the ground with other people, both off-balance and both adding weight that may, sooner or later, be irreversible. It's never quite as black and white as that, at one point or another everybody is going to be in that chair, weighted down and everybody will be surrounded with people to make a choice. Some are loyal soldiers that'll pick you up and take most of the weight, whilst this is appealing, it's not always the best choice at that time. Others are like roses that are full of colour and life yet covered in thorns that are just going to hurt and start to wilt, taking you down with them. And then sometimes, all it takes is a small glimpse of what balance looks like and someone to help you up to realise that the soldiers and the roses can co-exist in the same field in equal measure. However, the sad truth is, sometimes the roses need to be cut down because they are just too heavy. Sometimes, until you take inventory and realise what might actually be weighing you down, you'll never regain balance.

As the sound of the morning slowly faded into focus and light streamed through the gap in the curtains, my eyes opened and was once again greeted with the familiar sight of the mousy brown hair on the back of Chris' head. In my drunken reverie, I was unable to tell when he had finally walked through the door. My mouth was dry and the taste of residual wine coated my tongue. As I sat up, my head felt like it had inflated, clutching my forehead, I let out a subtle groan. I took a moment to steady myself, leaning backwards on one arm reaching for my phone to check the time. It was close to 8:00 a.m. and as I shuffled out of bed, Chris made no movements. I stared at his closed eyes and could only think about the level of peace he was at and that at any moment I could ruin that. It was then that I decided to leave the room and make coffee as I did every morning.

The living room was exactly as I had left it the night before. The table remained set with everything where I had left it. The bottle of wine was opened and I could see the leftover droplets pooling in the bottom of the glass. The note I left had shifted and the cling film that covered the leftover dinner had been disturbed slightly. Instinctively, I moved the plate to the fridge and turned the kettle on. As the water began to bubble, my mind shifted and I moved back towards the table. The bottle of wine had already been opened, what was another one or two sips, if for no other reason than to quench my thirst and put the headache at bay? Chris wouldn't notice and I could drink my coffee and brush my teeth before he had even woken up. The glass stood empty with only a few drops left in the bottom, I emptied them into my mouth and took the bottle in my other hand. Placing the glass in the sink, I opened the bottle and stopped. I began to trace back my steps to the night before, the first bottle, where had I put that? As the panic began to set in and the usual questions raced through my mind, I placed the bottle to my lips and drank as much in one go as my body could handle. I remained conscious of the volume, however, as to not rouse suspicion; a trick of the trade that is base addiction.

Guilt makes us react in two ways, it can make us run away and force blame on the blameless or it can force to love harder than we thought was even possible. The problem with the former, is that although it can be the easiest (and most common) route, running away from who you are will always be hard. That morning I had chosen the latter, the road less travelled that was paved with attentiveness and a sickly-sweet demeanour. Breakfast in bed said that loud and clear. Before approaching the baron fridge to scrape together whatever I could, that would accompany the predictable cup of tea, I took one last, long gulp of wine before placing it inside the fridge. My mind re-traced all the possible steps that I could remember from the night before, I checked the bin for an empty bottle, I checked under the sofa and between the cushions and I even stepped out on to the balcony to see if I'd thrown it over; no luck. Had I left it out and had Chris found it when he came home? Had he already thrown it away to pretend he hadn't noticed? Was he keeping it as ammunition? All were possible and daunting questions that I asked myself as I feebly began making scrambled eggs. I re-boiled the kettle and made tea as the wine began to fill my head again, my coffee had cooled by this point and I drank it down in one. In my mind, the smell of coffee was greater than that of wine. As I watched the steam rise, I took a deep breath and closed my eyes, trying to visualise an empty bottle, where I could have stashed it. A smile presented itself on my face, almost uncontrollably, like the night before even though inside I was beginning to panic. I placed Chris's breakfast on a tray before shaking off any residual guilt I was feeling and snagged the note from the night before, placing it in front of his mug of tea.

"I thought you could use it, enjoy!" the words written messily in black and white stared at me, unemotional and disconnected. Without further hesitation, I let the smile take over, natural and inconspicuous as I took the guilt-feast to the bedroom. When I opened the door, it was as if he hadn't moved since I left him, he remained still and quiet. His face was soft and peaceful and as he opened one eye to me standing with tea he began to smile. No words were exchanged because they didn't need to be; he sat up and took the tray from me, kissing me with one hand on my cheek. I was a part of his peace and just as thoughtlessly I could take it away, or I could force blame on the blameless. I could try to rationalise my reckless behaviour perhaps even turn the tables, blame it on a feeling of neglect even. That wasn't right and it wasn't going to happen in this perfect moment that I had un-intentionally crafted. Now that the alcohol had settled and the guilt was presented with a smile. I had no choice but to play the part of the doting housewife.

"Good morning!" I spoke faintly, almost a whisper that was made for his ears only. With one swift movement, I moved to my side of the bed, agile and soft as to not disturb the tray. Chris took his cup of tea and took a long sip, saying nothing.

"I've already had something," I lied, gesturing to his plate, sitting upright and quiet. The admission of 'something' somehow felt like less of a lie. I'd had a coffee and a glass or two of wine so technically 'something' was correct. He picked up his breakfast and began to eat, his voice was hoarse and he let out a faint, barely audible "thank you." He was uncharacteristically quiet and I assumed it was because of his previous long day, besides, I was playing the part of the understanding carer, not the paranoid lover so I said nothing and reached for my phone. It wasn't on the bedside table as it usually was but I could see the charging cable trailing from the wall to somewhere on the floor. I remained on the bed and followed the wire blindly with my hand until I felt the chill of the metallic device. With my fingers outstretched, I blindly lifted the phone from the floor until I felt a slight tug. The wire was caught forcing me to hang my head over the edge. I saw the bottle, it was empty and clear. It once held wine; with a sigh of relief, I lifted my phone as if nothing had happened. There was an element of comfort, that my drunk self still protected me from reality but it was nothing compared to the fear of loss and truth that could have turned everything upside down. I simply picked up the phone and continued as normal.

"You had me worried last night," I said, scrolling through the contact list in my phone carefully selecting Alex. He continued to eat and shuffled in his space glancing in my direction. I began a text message, carefully crafted deceit to give the impression that I was ill and unable to talk over the phone. As good as I had become at lying about myself, there were still certain skills I hadn't mastered, faking sick was not one of them. Nonetheless, I assured him I'd be back in the morning, ready to pick up where I'd left off. Chris finished his last mouthful and I turned my phone over, placing it on the bed beside me. As he placed his plate on the floor beside him, he turned to me, grabbing my hands pulling me down onto the bed with him. We laid facing each other, our noses inches away from one another and as he smiled, I could see there was something hidden behind it.

"We just got held up and I wasn't able to charge my phone. Thanks for dinner though, it was the perfect end to an otherwise shit day," he joked, still smiling. I didn't smile back.

"I thought as much. Why? you don't have another secret boyfriend I should know about do you?" I laughed. All things considered, it would have been the perfect poetic justice if he did.

"Listen," he whispered, encasing my hands in his "They need me to go away for a while."

"How long is a while?"

"Just a few weeks, we'll be going to Netherlands but I'm sort of left with no choice," he sounded apologetic, as if the news of him leaving me alone would be the worst that he could do. Maybe given the circumstances, to him, it would be.

I let out a short and breathy laugh, leaning in for a kiss and with a cheeky grin I replied "Thank god, I was about to retrieve my hunting gear."

"You'll be ok though, right?"

"Yes, I'll be fine. When do you have to go?" We both continued to smile at one another, still laying on the bed. I let go of his hands and placed one on the side of his stubbled face. I felt what I assumed to be a response to my text vibrate beside my leg. I sat up and opened up the message. As expected, it was a simple response, *That's ok, feel better soon.* My lie had worked. Simultaneously, Chris lifted his head and simply stated, "Two weeks."

"Well it's good I just got the day off then," I smiled, throwing my phone back down onto the bed.

"Well, what do we do with our suddenly free morning?" he grinned, sitting up right, fully turning to me. With a glint in his eye, he slowly lifted his shirt over his head, "Twice!" he winked, throwing his shirt to the floor crawling towards me. As his arms were stationed on either side of me, one hand slowly touched my cheek.

I laughed "Well, first I thought we could hoover and change the bedsheets, maybe scrub the floors or…" I was cut off by a hard and passionate kiss, the sort that once it was over you just wanted to hit rewind.

"Shut up!" he laughed and luckily, I hit rewind. As he grabbed my collar, the two of us still locked in our embrace, we fell onto the bed and began to undress each other. As our skin began to touch, the slight hair of his chest, the firm stomach and slight graze of stubble from his chin I could feel my heart beat against his. It was as if they were beating for each other, mine, then his in a syncopated rhythm that was followed by carefully choreographed hands through hair and fingers along waistlines. Two men, brought together, not as one but as individuals made for one another.

Once everything was over and the moment of clarity that usually follows climax began to wash over me, Chris gave me one last kiss before going off to retrieve a towel. I lay there, as I had done multiple times in the past, allowing the sweat

93

and heat to dissipate into the somewhat damp bed sheets, I ran a single hand through my sweat drenched hair. *"You'll be ok though, right?"* That's what he said. I replayed the words in the same masculine tone he had, I hadn't misheard or misinterpreted them, he had asked that exact question. Why now? Why this time? We had been apart before, in the past longer than two weeks and although a part of me knew it came with an air of concern my mind still had to ask, why now? In all the years we'd been together his work had always taken him away and I had made my peace with that albeit in the carefree self-destructive way that had led me to this point. I thought back to his first trip when the relationship was nothing but a few months old. He had pulled me from a life of repetitive empty dreams and within that few months we had both decided that we would give it our best.

I used to stare at him adoringly as everyone does with their first love. I'd had boyfriends before throughout school and such but there was something different about this one. My mind was cast back to the warm September afternoon that we first met. He stood tall and confident in a tight blue t-shirt, sunglasses hiding his eyes and shorts that showed off his toned calves. On his shoulder was a grey bag and, on his wrist, a cheap watch. First encounters are always awkward, especially for a fresh-faced seventeen-year-old like I was at the time. My hair was reminiscent of Justin Bieber and I wore what would become my signature knitted jumper and skinny jeans combo. I was the opposite, quiet and small and it wasn't until he noticed me that I even thought it was possible to have a conversation with a total stranger. That was the day that I learnt that everyone's a stranger until you make that contact. We made small talk and the scent of "Burberry Brit Rhythm" became the signature that he would forever sign across every encounter we were to have. Every time he'd pull me close after that day, I'd be reminded of the first time I smelt the oaky fresh scent and every day he wasn't around it was as if it never existed. I remember as the day moved forward that with every touch of the hand or sly smile, we were admitting that we didn't want the day to end.

Then it hit me, the towel Chris had retrieved from the bathroom landed directly over my face. Abruptly brought forward from reminiscing fondly of a time that seemed like an old tv show that was no longer in production. Why now? I asked again. I began to clean myself up as he sauntered around the room playfully teasing me with every step. As he carefully selected some immodest white underwear, he winked at me and crawled back into bed.

"I think I'm just going to grab a shower," I said, crawling over him, giving him one last kiss and allowing his hands to run down my back. I took the towel with me and returned his wink, once again finding myself in the bathroom, staring at the toilet. The wine was beginning to fade and although I knew there was nothing hidden where it usually was the instinct to check was all too natural. I stepped into the shower and as the water rained down on me, the night before began to replay. The sting of vodka, the stupid conversations with Andy and even the second trip for wine disguised as a loving gesture. I began to think back to before Chris and I had moved in together, back to when everything was still so fresh and new. A few months had passed from our first encounter, he took me to the city that we would eventually call home. I was seventeen. In the exciting city of London with someone I would have trusted with my life. I thought back to the night we spent in a hotel somewhere in Shoreditch when he finally asked me to be with him and I remember feeling that first flurry of passion that I hoped would never die. Thankfully, the next day he took me for a haircut and that awkward seventeen-year-old, whilst still present, was going to turn into something completely different.

I thought back to a few more months after that first night. I could say I was in a relationship, I had someone that I wanted to be with and that my friends liked. Someone who could hold my hand in the street or at a family dinner. We were sat in my parents' house on an old single bed when he cupped my hands in his, looked me in the eyes and gently said "Listen, work needs me to go a way for a while?"

"How Long?" I asked, my eyes dropping down.

"About a month, but you'll be ok though, right?" He whispered, using one hand to cup my chin, locking eye contact. I smiled and kissed him gently because I knew that I would.

The sound of a shower curtain being pulled back behind me snapped me out of my vision. I turned around to see his cheeky smile once again, "I did say twice," he beamed. I stopped for a moment, reliving every breath and kiss we had shared just moments prior, before pulling him under the shower "Wouldn't want to make you a liar!" I said.

The next day things returned to normal and I returned to work. Two weeks was long enough for us to enjoy many more days like the one we had just shared, besides the fact if I didn't at least try to make things better whilst I was still being reminded why I was here in the first place then there would be no point in trying at all. Yes, I had a momentary lapse, I had slipped off the wagon and well and truly let the wagon get away from me, but no one got hurt and I didn't do anything Earth-shattering this time. All I wanted to do was put it back away. As I stood in the shop, doing my day to day paperwork, Alex was off somewhere, probably smoking or attempting to flirt with a security guard, my mind began to wander again. *"You'll be ok though, right?"* the words continuously echoed in my mind and for some reason the question wouldn't stop repeating itself.

I thought back to the first time he had asked it, on the bed in my parents' house those few years ago. I remembered how I didn't need to answer because I knew I would but this time was different, something about those words just wouldn't stop looping over and over again. Another memory began to slip through, with the question still echoing. I woke up one morning, Chris had been gone for a few weeks and everything was as it should have been. As I opened my eyes, the morning seeped through as it did every day in the tiny box room of my parents' house. My bare feet met with the wooden looking linoleum and as everyone in a long-distance relationship does, I instantly reached for my phone. As expected, his name was the first I saw and I instantly smiled. I opened the message and began to read and as I scrolled through the ominous green bubble my entire body began to sink.

"I'm sorry but we can't be together anymore as I've been unfaithful whilst out here!" it read. I didn't read much further and the memory of the rest was blurred however, the memory of the earth shattering feeling of what could be described as a first broken heart is something that never leaves you. In that moment, it's as if all of your organs are made of glass and each one has splintered and cracked. I remember frantically responding asking to talk about it as any forlorn teenager would do. After a day of silence and pure torture, I felt nothing. I mourned for something that I thought could be real or was meant to be right. He was due home in a week or two and that desperate part of me knew if I could just talk to him it could be fixed. The next day he sent me another text and after crying myself to sleep, my teary eyes could barely make out the words, much less believe them.

"I want to see you when I get back, I can't live without you!" they read. Even at that tender age, there was a part of me that was hardened and if it were only out of spite, to tell him to go fuck himself. But we know that's not what happened. Even though it was resolved that feeling would always serve as a reminder.

As I began to slowly slip from the memory, the initial question began to fade away, guilt took its place. If Chris were to find out all of my hidden secrets and traits, he would be made to feel like I did on that day. Maybe I was subconsciously trying to justify my actions, maybe I wanted that somewhere in the deepest, darkest recesses of my mind and if that were true, I couldn't let it win. Perhaps all these years he'd been trying to make up for it, blissfully unaware that it was me who could hurt him. That's the problem when you stare at someone through rose coloured glasses, all the red flags just look like flags.

My train of thought was pulled incontinently from its tracks with a simple phrase. A familiar, deep voice spoke at me. I moved my eyes up from the counter.

"Hello you."

# Chapter 11
## *Track 11 – New Found Land – What Is Love?*

Wikipedia defines a sanctuary, in its original meaning, 'a sacred place, such as a shrine'. By the use of such places as a haven, by extension the term has come to be used for any place of safety. This secondary use can be categorised into human sanctuary, a safe place for humans, such as a political sanctuary; and non-human sanctuary, such as an animal or plant sanctuary. However, the word *sanctuary* in itself resonates with everyone in different ways depending on the circumstances we find ourselves in. It may have some strong connotations of a certain hunched bell-ringer, but no. For some of us, sanctuary is a person, it's a hug after a long day's work and it is an embrace in the middle of a depressive episode that makes it feel as though all of the broken pieces of yourself are going to be squeezed together. For some of us, sanctuary is a warm bed and a favourite film with a friend, it's a shoulder to cry on or a joke that makes your sides hurt. Sometimes sanctuary is an act, it's a cigarette or it's found at the bottom of a bottle.

Safety is a matter of perspective. We as people are able to lie so freely to ourselves that we feel safe when in fact the sanctuary that we think we've built for ourselves is actually the opposite of that. It's very easy to believe that something we have built for ourselves is the safest bet, but from the outside looking in, the walls of this haven that you've built for yourself may in fact be more like bars. A sanctuary, as easily as it is built, can be turned into a prison. The warmth turns cold and the shoulder to cry on turns to stone and the embrace is no longer comforting; it's suffocating. When this happens, where do you go? Where can you call your safe place now?

Of course, as dramatic as it may be, at some point, we have all experienced something that once made us feel so good and pure turn into something entirely different, malicious and dark, even. When this happens, it's so easy to turn to things that we can find within the former walls that we used to feel safe in, in order to feel safe again. But the truth is, you'll never find sanctuary at the bottom of the bottle because no matter how big the neck, there's no shoulder to cry on. These behaviours and habits that we can fall into come so naturally when it feels like our world has been flipped upside down that we can rob ourselves of the truth. It's hard to have your sanctuary turn into a prison, but it's even harder to see it for what it is and say 'no more'. It's harder to refuse to be the victim of circumstance and realise that the bars were never locked; this 'prison' is just an open cage. You can exit as easily as you entered.

Sometimes we're forced from the sanctuary and it can become someone else's. You can be pushed outside of the walls unwillingly and no matter how hard you fight, it doesn't belong to you anymore. In these instances, it's harder to give up and come to terms with the idea that the shoulder is no longer yours and someone else is having their broken pieces put together in your place. What's easy, is to tell yourself that you'll never let yourself into another safe haven so long as you shall live. It's easy to create your own prison around yourself and really lock the door behind you. But that is no way to live and that is no way to love; build as many sanctuaries as you can. As many safe havens and shrines that you can manage, there will always be another shoulder and another embrace that'll feel just as safe if not safer than the ones before. It is no way to live, to wait to love. Failing that, bad habits will always be just that, habits to fall back on when all else fails.

I looked up from my work to follow the familiar voice and as they slowly trailed up to see the face behind the familiarity my throat went dry. It was the familiar itch that I'd felt on so many occasions, the kind that could be scratched by a simple clear bottle. His eyes met with mine and the natural smile that came with the retail territory quickly faded into a dull and blank expression. I turned cold before speaking slowly, "How can I help you today, sir?" I spoke, soft and dry as I had done to every customer before, even though this wasn't a customer. John stared back at me, hair perfectly shaped, suit perfectly pressed as it always had been. He smiled back. I clenched my jaw, bit my tongue and refrained from saying all the words that in any other instance I would have been free to vocalise. If he was going to get to me, he had chosen the right battle ground, I was trapped behind a counter and behind a simple retail worker; one false move and not only would I jeopardise my sanity and ability to take the high ground but my job.

"I just thought I'd come and see what was on offer," he spoke.

"Unfortunately, we have no special deals today, although we have a new range of items perfect for *children.*" I smiled leaning over the counter, inches away from the other side. It was the only power move I had to play and, in that moment, I saw his eyes shift, perhaps he had chosen the right battlefront after all. I could see Alex in the distance wandering towards the shop, apparently the security guards wouldn't bite but a Starbucks was what he'd settled on. John looked over his shoulder and saw where my eyes were locked; I grinned, still glassy eyed.

"Look, I just want to talk, you know where I'll be," he whispered.

"Have a nice day sir!" I falsely chimed just as Alex entered and he left, smiling just as fake as he always had.

"What was he after?" Alex said, approaching me with a coffee, looking John up and down with no discretion.

"He was just asking if we had something. I told him he needs to go round the corner," I shrugged, moving to my knees placing the paperwork below the counter. He stood beside me, staring at the storefront with no movement.

"Wasn't he the cute daddy from the other day?" he joked as I looked him dead in the eye. He gave me a wink as I rose up from the floor.

"I have no idea who that man is," I stared at the door, "And shut the fuck up, please never use that phrase again. You're disgusting!" I laughed, playfully nudging him with my fist. My laughter acted as a mask, he didn't know the truth behind the words. As I continued to look at the door frame, I couldn't concentrate on anything other than the fact that this man would be round the corner, waiting for me. I knew it was wrong, in the deepest recesses of my mind, I screamed out "*don't go, let sleeping dogs lie!*" but it's not as simple as that.

Isaac Newton once said that 'Every action has an equal and opposite reaction', for every up there is a down, every stop there is a go, every backwards there is a forward and you get the idea. But what if that reaction to your actions becomes a conflict? A conflict between action and reaction and if you were in the contradicting throws of these two emotions how would you ever choose? I've come to realise that maybe it's not about choosing as much as it is just living with it. We can feel both at the same time, sometimes we can feel a reaction in the midst of a loving action and there's no explanation for it. Sometimes the conflict is with one's self, can you love yourself if you don't know who that is? Can you make the right choice if you've never been shown how?

"I'm going for a break, is that ok?" I asked, mostly from courtesy because in that moment, I knew I was leaving and where I was going. I didn't wait for his response and I didn't hesitate. I left the shop and marched toward the corner; I knew he would be there. As I walked from the shop, everything went silent. I had a pre-rehearsed script of everything I wanted to say, I wanted to vocalise how disgusted I was and how angry I could be. I practiced, on loop, the words that would shut everything down for a few minutes. I saw him, stood in a darkened doorway, as I approached. He smiled, the toothy grin that first caught me, in that moment, I saw every past fling and thought to myself; "How was I going to get out of it?" I suppose, I thought perhaps I'd get closure, perhaps, he could explain himself, give an excuse even, but choosing between something comfortable and wrong and comfortable and *right* is easier said than done. As I moved forward, it became clear, perhaps I didn't have to 'get out of it' but maybe I could use it, the way I'd been used. He knew my weaknesses and I knew his. As if like clockwork, he reached into his satchel as I arrived just a few feet in front of him. A long, thin, glassy neck peered tauntingly from beneath the folds. It was no longer a question of "*how* I was going to get out of it?" but rather "*What was* I going to get out of this?" and I already knew that.

"Don't say a fucking word you miserable, foul and spineless old man!" I said with gritted teeth, staring him directly in the eye. His hand lowered, the bottle disappearing back into the bag. He saw my eyes follow it and I saw the cogs working in his mind. He smiled again.

"I said talk, not fight!" holding up his arms with his palms outstretched.

"I bought you a gift, a peace offering."

"What I want, you can't afford!" I deepened my tone, daring to move closer. Before he responded, he removed the satchel from his shoulder and put it over my arm. I felt the weight of what was inside.

"Oh?" he laughed "Take a look, I bet even you can still be surprised," he joked.

I glared at him and curiously draped the bag open, inside was the expected bottle of vodka. Through the clear glass, I could see a white rectangle, distorted by the alcohol. Moving the bottle to the side I pulled what was now clearly an envelope upward.

"What's this? A handwritten apology? An explanation?" I argued as I pulled the envelope out into plain site.

"Take it, if you don't want it, you know where to return it." He said finally, before he pushed passed me and back down the street, leaving the satchel on my shoulder and the envelope in my hands and even more questions.

# Chapter 12
## *Track 12 – Hozier – Shrike*

Everyone tries to do the right thing. The right thing is a matter of perspective for most people and sometimes the lines can be blurred as to exactly what the right thing is. You're going to be surrounded by people who have their own opinions on exactly what the right thing is, however, you are the only one who can decide exactly what that is and as a result make a conscious decision to act upon it. Bottom line is we all try to do the right thing and this is easier when life is going well for us and we're feeling okay. These are the times when we tend to take care of ourselves properly, spend time in other people's company, stay active and keep out of trouble. It's at times like these when doing the right thing is a lot easier because it doesn't even need to be a conscious choice, it just comes naturally.

But it can be harder when life isn't going so well, or at least what we perceive as not going so well. You just got dumped, you've made a mistake in your job and now they've put you on a performance plan or your car breaks down in the middle of a dirt road the day before payday. Someone who you thought you could trust has betrayed that and it feels like nobody wants anything to do with you or you simply missed the train and your career now hangs in the balance because you'll be late for that very important meeting; whatever it is that makes it seem like life is going south, in these instances, doing the right thing can become increasingly difficult. It's in these times when life is not going so well that we can all start falling into patterns of behaviour that really don't help us at all. In fact, they only make things harder for us. It can feel like someone has pulled the rug out from underneath you except instead of falling and hitting the ground, you'll just keep falling until you can no longer see the surface.

We might let ourselves go, or shut ourselves away from everyone, stop doing things we enjoy, or maybe even get into real trouble and none of these behaviours are going to do anything to help resolve the life we've deemed lacking or difficult. When people lose things, such as respect or dignity, love and trust or even themselves the behaviours we exhibit in search of the right thing tend to do the complete opposite. It's so easy to sit in the dark underneath a pile of clothes and binge watch Netflix for three days. It's easy to drink until you pass out and it's easy to ignore absolutely every piece of advice you receive from the friends and family that definitely surround you. It's easy, when feeling like this, to simply let time slip away. Letting our time slip away just makes it even easier to make the wrong choices, makes us more likely to lapse into unhealthy behaviours. Where problems can really start is when we get up each day and let the time just slip away without doing anything useful with it. When doing nothing becomes the routine, you're left with nothing and that lack of fulfilment just becomes greater and what else are you going to do with your time other than fill that void with something that's just going to make things worse.

If we don't have any proper structure or routine in our day, we can find ourselves drifting and doing nothing much at all. When we don't do anything and that lack of fulfilment grows, the guilt grows with it and it's when we feel bored, empty, lonely or low then it becomes easier to make the complete wrong choice. Whatever your vice may be, whether that's casual sex, fast food, drugs or alcohol, it's in times like these when it's all the more tempting to turn to them. Some people simply aren't built to be bored or alone. As it's been said before, alcohol is a lubricant and you can use it then to slowly fuck yourself, and this goes for every unhealthy vice or coping mechanism you may have developed. We simply can't feel good if we do nothing that we deem fun or worthwhile.

If we never do anything enjoyable then it's very easy to start having gloomy thoughts about our lives and the situation, we're in. And if we never do anything that makes us feel we've achieved something worthwhile, how can we expect to build up our confidence and feel proud of ourselves? Some will tell you that pride is a sin, but I say screw those people, you should be allowed to feel proud of everything you've done, even if it's as simple as taking a shower today, changing your bed sheets or staying sober for a week. When you manage to do the right thing, it should be celebrated.

It's easier said than done, to try to plan ahead and put structure in our days (and more importantly stick to it) but it's something that's needed because as I've mentioned before, the human brain has an incredible talent for tearing itself to pieces. No one will do it for you and it's a skill that you have to learn for yourself, planning your time and putting some structure into your days is so important in aiding the conscious choices to do the right thing. If you can get into a routine of regularly doing things you enjoy and things that give you a feeling of success, that's a very positive strength to have. It's all about replacing those negative behaviours with positive influences and actions that can strip the guilt of doing nothing away. Do something to be proud of, do something fun or adventurous, but more importantly, do it for yourself.

Alcoholism, for me, was the need to have something there constantly. I had become dependent on Chris and his guidance. I had become dependent on the next drink that I knew was just around the corner. As the satchel that sat on my shoulder began to weigh down on me, I slipped the envelope back beneath the bottle, forgetting its existence entirely. As I approached the shop front, I could see Alex waiting behind the counter, his smile and eager eyes looking me up and down with what could only be described as unwanted lust.

"New bag?" he asked, beady eyes and full of intrigue. I immediately pushed passed him, making brief eye contact before smiling slightly.

"Yeah, it was on sale, how could I consciously leave it, looks good, no?" I toyed with him, pretending to model it as though to not arouse suspicion. I flirtatiously turned to the left and then to the right, using my hand to shield the real weight of what was inside before exiting to the stockroom. I left the bag behind and continued the day.

Once the day came to a close, Alex made his usual jokes and I made an excuse that I would have to get a later train. Any excuse to leave. As I left the shop, the satchel hit me in the leg and I was reminded of the gift I'd been given earlier on, as I opened the bag, I was reminded of the gift that John had left. The red cap and the clear alcohol moved back and forth like a river that's ebb and flow was carrying me away. The walk to the train station that day seemed to take longer than usual with every step the weight became more apparent and with every inch closer to the entrance my thoughts became more blurred. I had done the right thing leaving the shop when I did, I had done the right thing biting my tongue and acting calm as John badgered me like a witness in court but had I done the right thing keeping the bag in the first place? Was I going to do the right thing now by returning it? After all, as he rightly pointed out, I knew where to return it.

There's always going to be a boundary to push. Throughout every stage of our lives, boundaries are put in place and dictated by others. Social boundaries are put in place by our parents and educational boundaries by the teachers at school and when we enter the world of work, professional boundaries become the very foundation of a career. The boundaries of love and lust get thrown at us from the very first time we look at someone and feel those butterflies in our stomach, however, for some of us, the boundaries become blurred and simply beg to be pushed. The first time you have an argument with your parents or misbehave at school you begin to test them. I had mastered the art of pushing a boundary just far enough that it wouldn't break but it would just get wider. They would get more ambiguous and less clear. Before I could choose, I consciously found myself on the wrong platform at the station. Boarding the train that wouldn't take me home but somewhere that I might not return from-a new boundary that was unexplored but that was willing to be pushed.

I had planned to do the right thing. I had planned to walk right up to John's door, drop the bag outside and go home, I would make an excuse to Chris that I had to stay late for one reason or another and then I could try and fix everything else. As I walked through the corridor that was all too familiar, edging closer towards his door, the satchel moving from side to side seemingly becoming heavier and heavier with every step. As I stood a few feet from the door, I could see a light from inside seeping through the cracks. Holding my breath, silent and still, I opened the bag and took one last look at the bottle. This whole story had started with a bottle and I could end it here in the same way, do the right thing, leave it on the floor and walk away. Then it caught my eye, the white rectangular shape at the bottom, distorted by the moving alcohol. I removed the bottle, then the envelope. A letter perhaps? The right thing in that moment would have been to leave both by the door and catch the soonest train home but as I continued to feel the paper between my fingers, the curiosity became overwhelming. After all, this boundary was as thin as the seal on the envelope, what harm could it really do? Holding the bottle between my fingers, I tore open the envelope. My eyes widened as I removed a small stack of papers kept together with a small paperclip. I let the empty envelope fall to the floor as I read the small slip of paper at the top of the stack "I'm sorry!" it read, scrawled neatly in thick black ink. Beneath the initial scrap followed a fifty-pound note and beneath that what looked like about fifteen, maybe twenty others all clipped together neatly. As I stood there with the money in one hand and the cheap vodka in the other, my instincts kicked in and before I could think about them, I began taking a long and hard gulp from the bottle. As I did, the light flickered behind the door as someone approached. I threw the money back into the bag and took off in the opposite direction, back down the corridor as fast as I could manage.

*"What was this?"* I thought as I ducked around the corner, hearing the faint sound of a door opening behind me. As I entered on to the street, I took one last gulp from the bottle before replacing it in the bag on my shoulder. Was this any apology? Was this hush money? Or was it some twisted pay off that would keep me on his side like an employee? I hadn't returned it and I had already began drinking his other 'gift' so whatever it was or was meant to be I had accepted it. It was beginning to get dark as I reached the station. As I stepped onto the platform, I turned my phone off, at least this way, I wouldn't be forced to lie. Chris would ask where I'd been and I could say my phone died and the train was delayed. As I boarded the first available train, I noticed the car was eerily quiet, I noticed a young girl was sitting a few rows behind me reading an old copy of Charlotte Brontë's *Jane Eyre* as I consciously made the choice to sit with my back to her. As we started moving along the tracks with the ongoing scenery passing by as one continuous blur, passing through tunnels and other stations, I took another drink. The girl behind me paid no mind as far as I was aware. I could hear unintelligible music playing through her headphones as she calmly turned a page.

I remembered reading the very same book in school once. It became poignant in my mind as it began to fog up with alcohol. Towards the beginning of the book, Brontë writes:

*"My mind made its first earnest effort to comprehend what had been infused into it concerning heaven and hell: and for the first time it recoiled, baffled; and for the first time glancing behind, on each side, and before it, it saw all around an unfathomed gulf: it felt the one point where it stood – the present; all the rest was formless cloud and vacant depth: and it shuddered at the thought of tottering , and plunging amid that chaos."*

Perhaps that's what I was doing; considering what I knew of heaven and hell, or what I had thought of it, on this very train, I was moving through the chaos that had engulfed my life. As the train began to pull into the next station, I heard the girl pack her belongings and begin to move towards the door. In a panicked rush I took another sip, not knowing who may jump on in her place. She moved beside my seat as the automated voice announced our arrival at the station, telling us to be mindful of the doors and to let others off before boarding. I had managed to drink, undetected, as she turned to me and smiled before leaving into the crowd, holding her book. Had she gotten to that section yet? I wondered as I kept an eye on the doors. This time, a businessman in a sharp suit boarded, brief-case in hand.

Now there was a man on the train, he sat and he minded his own business in silence. My mind drifted off as I took another sip. There was a man on the train and he was trying to prove something to his friends by bragging about the many conquests he'd had that weekend. There was also a man who didn't think anything at all, he sat in silence and judged as I drank but he let me go about my day. There was a man on the train that worried about his relationship, he was concerned that he wasn't loved by everyone he loves and there was s also a man that was stewing in his regrets. My mind thought of every man this man could be and every one of them I was to him.

There's always someone, somewhere, wherever you look that's thinking and calculating just waiting to be recognised or ignored. As a functioning member of society, it's our job to figure out which one. My point is, that everyone, no matter how big or small, is doing their own thing. I began to realise that everyone is concerned about their own lives and everyone is affected to that end. I had a teacher when I was in secondary school and she said something that resonated with me in that moment; "everyone's problems seem big and important to them because they are their own." I had gotten into this mess and maybe some people would have no problem at all carrying the weight of the money and everything that came with it.

Everyone is dealing with something and they all have something they're going through, so why should what I was doing to myself give me the right to carry on as if everything was normal? I thought back to the girl and to everything I knew of heaven and hell. What did I know? Was this train taking me home or in to further trouble? I couldn't help but look at the man reading his paper, was he a good person? Would he be joining me to my destination of more trouble? Did he notice me at all as I took another drink, and another with each station we passed and every tunnel we went through. I lifted feet and rested them on the vents beside my seat, my boots making a slight squeak as they adjusted. In that moment, I smiled. *"I'm the man on the train, I'm going to sit in silence and calculate"* I thought, moving the bottle towards my lips. The train began to slow down and I could see the station outside. It was time for me to leave. There was a man on the train and he opened his eyes, he realised that being alone was better than faking it and being drunk was easier than being sober.

I was now two different people. There was the man on the train who was invisible and could drink freely with no consequences. The observer that could pass judgement, the same man that passed through the clockwork beehive and saw people for who they really were and the person who felt no guilt and didn't second guess my choices. I was the bad man that made all the wrong choices and continued to do so; the man that people told they preferred sober but, in my mind, did everything they could to make it untrue. I would tell myself that these boundaries had been pushed by someone else and the other person I was, the one who was sober and over-thought every conversation or every word, was forced into being.

As I left the train and stumbled towards my home, I passed an old derelict building next to a bus stop. I had never paid much attention to the house before but for some reason, the house seemed inviting, as if it was challenging me. I thought of everything, of John and of Chris and of every time that I had felt just like this house. Abandoned and forgotten, I took one last sip before throwing the empty bottle into the bushes. As I approached the flat, I became overwhelmed with guilt, I had been drinking all day, how was I going to return from this? Chris would know because he always knew, whether or not he said so, but guilt makes people react in strange ways.

I approached the front door, shaking with my mind clouded in alcohol, I attempted to place my key in the lock. As the key scratched against the wood, trying to locate the lock, the door opened. Chris stood, broad shouldered and unphased by my state, as he had done before. His eyes locked with mine as I stood crouched and bleary eyed, still holding the key in place of the lock. I smiled, laughed a little as he retreated into the living room.

# Chapter 13
## *Track 13 - Nitesky*
## *- Robot Koch*

Wikipedia defines a sanctuary, "in its original meaning, is a sacred place, such as a shrine. By the use of such places as a haven, by extension the term has come to be used for any place of safety. This secondary use can be categorised into human sanctuary, a safe place for humans, such as a political sanctuary; and non-human sanctuary, such as an animal or plant sanctuary." However, the word *sanctuary* in itself resonates with everyone in different ways depending on the circumstances we find ourselves in. It may have some strong connotations of a certain hunched bell-ringer, but no. For some of us, sanctuary is a person, it's a hug after a long day's work and it is an embrace in the middle of a depressive episode that makes it feel as though all of the broken pieces of yourself are going to be squeezed together. For some of us, sanctuary is a warm bed and a favourite film with a friend, it's a shoulder to cry on or a joke that makes your sides hurt. Sometimes sanctuary is an act, it's a cigarette or it's found at the bottom of a bottle.

Safety is a matter of perspective. We as people are able to lie so freely to ourselves that we feel safe when in fact the sanctuary that we think we've built for ourselves is actually the opposite of that. It's very easy to believe that something we have built for ourselves is the safest bet, but from the outside looking in, the walls of this haven that you've built for yourself may in fact be more like bars. A sanctuary, as easily as it is built, can be turned into a prison. The warmth turns cold and the shoulder to cry on turns to stone and the embrace is no longer comforting; it's suffocating. When this happens, where do you go? Where can you call your safe place now?

Of course, as dramatic as it may be, at some point we have all experienced something that once made us feel so good and pure turn into something entirely different, malicious and dark, even. When this happens it's so easy to turn to things that we can find within the former walls that we used to feel safe in, in order to feel safe again. But the truth is, you'll never find sanctuary at the bottom of the bottle because no matter how big the neck, there's no shoulder to cry on. These behaviours and habits that we can fall into come so naturally when it feels like our world has been flipped upside down that we can rob ourselves of the truth. It's hard to have your sanctuary turn into a prison, but it's even harder to see it for what it is and say 'no more'. It's harder to refuse to be a victim of circumstance and realise that the bars were never locked; this 'prison' is just an open cage. You can exit as easily as you entered.

Sometimes we're forced from the sanctuary and it can become someone else's. You can be pushed outside of the walls unwillingly and no matter how hard you fight, it doesn't belong to you anymore. In these instances, it's harder to give up and come to terms with the idea that the shoulder is no longer yours and someone else is having their broken pieces put together in your place. What's easy is to tell yourself that you'll never let yourself into another safe haven so long as you shall live. It's easy to create your own prison around yourself and really lock the door behind you. But that is no way to live and that is no way to love; build as many sanctuaries as you can. As many safe havens and shrines that you can manage, there will always be another shoulder and another embrace that'll feel just as safe if not safer than the ones before. There is no way to live, to wait to love.

"I'm Sorry!" I mumbled, slurring my words as I had done before, feebly following Chris into the flat. I could see in his eyes that he was disappointed and hurt but all I could think was the comforting embrace of another drink. It was a simple sentence. Seven letters, two words but what did it mean? For some, an empty apology just rolled off the tongue and for others, it's almost impossible to admit any wrongdoing, it's not admissible or even a possibility. Seven single letters and two simple words that can change your entire perspective overnight. How could I dictate when Chris should decide to believe them? I had already given him multiple reasons not to. How could I ask him to be okay with just those two words? I followed him up the stairs and into our bedroom.

As I pushed the door open after him, my eyes were focused on trying to remain sober as possible. He stood, silent for a moment, staring directly at me, before his voice could barely be heard as a whisper, "Why?" he asked.

It was then that I realised he was gesturing to the bed, an empty bottle of wine, an empty bottle of gin and the empty bottle I thought I had thrown over the balcony, all laid out in front of me like some photo album of deceit. I said nothing and stood in silence.

"I thought you were getting better. I thought we were fixing this," he said dejectedly.

"We? We weren't fixing anything. This is down to me, this is mine. You're leaving, again and I will be fine, you've made sure of that. I'm so sorry, I can't explain it!" I begged. My voice began to tremble, maybe it was the vodka, maybe it was the realisation that Chris was slipping away, regardless, a single tear began to roll down my cheek.

"Do you think I want to go away worrying about you every second? I hate that, I hate this. I hate that we've become a couple that's comfortable lying to each other," he argued. The tears immediately stopped. The words echoed in my drunken mind, *"Lying to each other"* what had he lied to me about?

"What does that mean?" I retorted defensively, removing my bag and jacket, throwing them on to the bed. He stood in front of me, not moving, staring at me as I tried to focus.

"Nothing, I just mean that maybe time apart is what we need. I can't handle going away and knowing you're like this. I can't do anything from the other side of the world," he replied, his voice steady and unwavering. "I leave tomorrow," he said.

"Please, I thought we had more time," I muttered drunkenly.

In certain sub-cultures cannibals only eat the enemies they admire. They do this in order to take in all the qualities that make them stronger or better. Maybe the same can be said for the ones we love. Maybe we only love people in an attempt to make ourselves better. We've all heard the term "Opposites attract" but perhaps it's more than that, opposites attract because we need each other otherwise we'll never find balance. I had learnt from Chris the ability to love unconditionally and now he was going to learn how to distrust those who you give your heart wholly to.

I stood in front of him, red with rage and before I could think the words started pouring.

"You'll be ok. I know you will," he said, looking to the ground as I looked to the ceiling. The tears filled my eyes as he cupped my neck with his large, rough hands. Pulling my focus forward, our foreheads touched and we locked eyes.

"That's because you're always ok," he whispered.

Was I? Had I become that much of a trickster that someone who claimed to know me better than anyone else could think that I was always ok? Or was it that I pretended so much that it had become normal?

"You don't get to do that. You don't get to go around, looking like that and acting so full of character meeting whoever you want, whenever you want," I began, the tears beginning to fill my eyes and tip over the lid. I pulled away.

"I know I'm a mess and I know it's easy for me to be your scapegoat. I know this isn't perfect and that you didn't ask for this, for me, but you can't do that. You can't make me love you and leave," I cried, stood inches from his face. As the tears began to roll down my cheeks, my vision became blurred, perhaps it was the vodka, perhaps it was the tears but all I wanted in that moment was for him to grab me and kiss me and make everything ok. I ran my hands through my hair, turning away as a feeble attempt to conceal my anger.

"I don't understand. I just don't know how you can stand there so silent and see that I want this, this, me and you and nothing else and I want to try and I want to be better and I want your help and you can just go," I whispered.

"I don't understand how you can just lie to me all this time and think nothing of it!" he yelled.

I flinched, stepping back a few paces, swaying in place as the vodka began to hit me.

"You're drunk now aren't you? I can't have a relationship with a bottle. I don't know who you are anymore," he spoke, his words sincere and cutting.

"Me neither," I whimpered. I leaned in close and as our lips met, he kissed me back one last time. Without another word, he pulled away and left the room. As the door closed, I fell to the floor. The tears fell to the carpet, leaving darkened spots as they fell. I heard the front door open and close behind him. In that moment, I felt like a new born that hadn't been around long enough to experience the hurt that was to follow. I acted like the victim when I had caused this. My hands reached beneath the mattress, feeling for the cold and comforting feel of a glass bottle. He had missed this one. As I felt the cold glass, I felt comfort and even though the hug I wanted wasn't going to be at the bottom I knew that I would rather feel nothing than the heartbreak or guilt or whatever feelings were swirling around in my head at the time. I took a long sip and laid back down on the floor.

A few hours later, I opened my eyes, still on the floor, the sun had set and the house was dark. I heard nothing but the sound of traffic in the street, immediately reaching for my phone, blinding myself with the light from the screen. No messages. As I sat up, I could see the empty bottles on the bed, he hadn't been home. It was midnight and I knew he was gone. As my hands reached out into the darkness, I found my bag, folded on the floor, and as I reached inside, I pulled the money John had given me from the bottom. As an instinct, I pulled the bottle from beneath the mattress and took another long drink. The vodka woke me up, almost, what was the point in hiding it. It was almost midnight and that meant nothing in a city that never sleeps. If Chris was going to leave, then so was I.

# Chapter 14

## *Track 14 – Beginners*
## *& Night Panda – Start a Riot*

Everyone's physical sensations ebb and flow all the time. We all have lots of physical sensations ebbing and flowing inside our body all the time, like the ocean tides or river and these can be affected by many different things. You may simply be hungry or you didn't sleep the previous night, what time of day it is or how much caffeine you've had or we've drunk. You could have some more literal feelings because you're just that clumsy or you're hungover. Sometimes we won't pay them any attention at all and even though they're still happening they have absolutely no impact on our day whatsoever. Other times, however, when we notice these sensations it can be easy to focus on them. When this happens and the tide rolls in it can feel like there's nothing but these feelings and nothing else matters.

Our physical sensations can be caused by our emotions. One of the most important and common causes of our physical sensations is our emotions, it's never a simple case of mind over matter. We each live with that tide inside of us that allows our emotions to dictate what we feel and when we feel it. For example, if we're feeling nervous, your stomach churns over and over and your muscles tense up or feeling butterflies in your stomach when you meet someone new. When you become angry or scared, your heart beats faster and you begin to shake almost uncontrollably, or if we're feeling down, that sense of heaviness inside your head and body becomes overwhelming and you begin to feel exhausted. Sometimes, the sadness hits in waves. The sensation is like a gust of wind that inexplicably blows on an otherwise calm day. It rises from your chest and resonates through to the tips of your fingers. It catches you unawares whilst on a train or watching your favourite tv show. It can make you feel completely alone in a crowded room. It too ebbs and flows like a river that wants to wash away any rationality that you were holding onto.

It's tempting to hold on to these thoughts and feelings, much like an addiction. You can get a cathartic sense of relief sometimes from letting those waves hit you because it's almost like if you're feeling sad, at least you're feeling something. With any addiction, however comes cravings and cravings can strike us without warning at any time. Whatever point in life we're at, the emotional cravings are the physical sensations that can really trouble us. Typically bought on by a drastic change and although these cravings are most likely to happen in the early stages of recovery, they can potentially strike at any time. This is because our feelings are often triggered by particular places, people or even hearing music that's linked in our minds to times we've had in the past. A certain film or song that holds so many memories that you can no longer see or hear it without feeling those waves crash down on you, almost ruining them for you.

This can then lead to powerful urges to lapse into whatever unhelpful behaviours we've picked up as a result of the previous waves we've dealt with before. For many of us, it's just a way to relieve these feelings. But this relief only ever lasts for a short time and as soon as we come crashing back down to reality, the feelings come flooding back and with them, a sense of disappointment. However, it's necessary to remind ourselves that it's not our fault that we feel the way we feel, acknowledge them and apologise for your actions as a result (where appropriate) and move on. After all, Frankenstein is to blame for creating the monster; not the monster itself for simply existing. The minute our negative coping mechanisms are over, the cravings will always come back – often even stronger than before. So by giving in, we just create more cravings and we set ourselves up to lapse yet again to get relief.

When the waves hit, the key is to stay strong and not give in to it. I know this is easier said than done and you don't necessarily need to ignore the feelings that are going to crash into you. Turn it around, ride the wave and instead of letting it wash over you, let it carry you back to normality. If you were happy every day of your life, you wouldn't be a person, you'd be a daytime television host; it's unreasonable to think that you can be. However, what *is* reasonable, is to know that any negativity doesn't need to be dealt with negatively. Once you can do that you'll no longer need to worry because you'll know you can stay strong and get over yourself more than anything. Remember, your bad days are just your good days on hold, they'll pick up eventually.

As I pulled myself from the floor and began to drink, I thought of every person that had contributed. I thought of the many ways I could get out or get them clear of my head. In that moment my mind switched, I held in one hand one thousand pounds and in the other, a bottle of vodka that cost no more than ten. As I finished the bottle, I moved to my wardrobe and discarded the empty glass on the bed to join the others. I grabbed an old white T-shirt and threw on a pair of ripped blue jeans. I grabbed my denim jacket and threw on my brown leather boots before heading down the stairs to the kitchen. I climbed upon the kitchen side and felt for the emergency cigarettes hidden atop the cupboard. I grabbed the packet, forcing them to the inside pocket. I checked my pockets for my keys and left my phone on the floor upstairs. I had decided if Chris could leave, so could I.

As I entered the underground, the clockwork beehive began to move once again. Everything as if choreographed and rehearsed. I thought back to the first time I had to travel to work alone and imagined myself amongst every person that was drunk and enjoying their night. I thought back to how I had pre-judged everyone the first time around. Did they know? Did people know that I was drunk? Was there another me slowly descending into the underground system judging me as I willingly moved towards what could essentially be my undoing?

Bees and wasps are categorised in the same subtext when referred to by people. Although biologically similar, the connotations associated with the two are completely different. One is seen as a docile friend and the other as an angry enemy that just wants to endanger and hurt you. Not many people know this but it's a common technique when harvesting honey to use smoke to make the bees more complacent and gentle, to not see anything as a threat and to accept their fate. Although, seen as a somewhat unethical practice, it works. Otherwise, the bees would attack those who they saw as invaders. Wasps, however, when exposed to nicotine, fly into a blind rage, a rage so intense that, eventually, they turn on themselves and turn their own stingers inward, completely self-destructing. The same can be said of people. We're all biologically similar but is the smoke we inhale going to make us complacent or angry? I was a wasp, and a beehive, clockwise or other, was no place for a wasp.

I was sat on the underground train, thinking of everything that had passed and as the sound air rushed through the tunnels of the underground system, my mind went blank. Finally, I was blank; I had no thoughts, no feelings, nothing that could define me as one way or the other. As I exited the clockwork beehive and as I entered on to the street, I felt overwhelmed by the lights and sounds. The distant noise of music beckoned me, I was in Vauxhall and knew where I was going in that moment. The music continued to play and I drunkenly showed my ID to the bouncer and went inside. Lights of red and green, blue and pink strobed as I made my way to the bar. I leant against the cold steel, looking at all of the available spirits. As I turned my head, I could see a man, perhaps two years older than me, not by much and as we locked eyes, he winked. I smiled, ordered my double vodka and coke and as the barman handed me my drink, the stranger slid him a five-pound note. He was rugged, well-muscled and wearing a tank top, his neatly trimmed beard told me all I needed to know. I looked him in the eye, a kind shade of green that the strobe lights and music normally wouldn't have let me see.

"Thanks!" I shouted, as the music had become too loud. I took my drink from the bartender, holding it up as if we were toasting each other, and moved towards the dance floor. He followed me. As the music played, his muscled body came closer to mine, he danced and I danced back, moving my body and drinking simultaneously. As I finished my drink and threw the plastic cup to the ground, we continued to dance, our sweaty bodies edging closer and closer. His biceps were smooth and firm, as my hands ran up to his broad shoulders his hand gripped my waist, pulling me into his body. I didn't know who he was but I was willing to find out. I could feel him against my body, his jeans were bulging and practically stiff against mine as we moved to the music. It was a repetitive techno-beat and the strobe lights had desensitised us to any form of rationality. He pulled me closer by the waist, our crotches touching and as the alcohol began to fill my mind, I felt him pressed against me. A stranger by any name that wasn't Chris's, I didn't know him and he didn't know me but I followed as his hand pulled mine towards the bathrooms. As we entered, I was thrust against a wall, his beard tickled as he kissed my neck up and down. I pushed back and I could see his muscles ripple as he locked his eyes on mine. There was a hunger and I felt it too. He stepped backwards into a cubicle and I followed without hesitation, immediately seeing a small plastic bag being pulled from his pocket.

He began pouring out what I could only assume was cocaine onto the toilet seat, removing from his back pocket a metal straw. As we both stood, mere inches away from each other in the one cubicle, he began using a card to make two smooth, clean lines on the seat. He handed me the straw and without delay, I pressed a nostril and snorted one of the lines. The burning sensation slowly trickled to the back of my throat and as I swallowed, he took the straw from me, sniffing the other line. His eyes widened as he passionately began to kiss me, with a raw sense of animalism. He began by kissing my neck all the while using his large hands to feel all over my body. The cocaine high began and as the chemical taste hit the back of my throat, I launched the attack. Pressing my tongue against his I began kissing the stranger with no thought other than continuing what I had started on the dance floor. His mouth was warm and as I ran my hands down his waist, feeling every notch and every bump in his denim jeans, finally and readily grabbing at what I could feel. There I was, without a word between us other than a drunken thank you, I let this stranger complete his mission. His lips kissed my neck as he pulled my jacket down, followed by my jeans. As he completed what we were there to do, I finished and he smiled. Immediately I was made to think of a speech I heard off-hand once, from a movie.

*"You are walking down a dock. There's a boat at the end of this dock and you get in the boat but you never notice that the boat is rotting and you can't drive this boat and now it's up to you to paddle. The boat starts sinking and you need to swim. You're drowning now…and you've hit bottom. Feel rock bottom. Now admit you never learned how to drive the boat and you never bothered to fix the rot. But this isn't the first boat you've been on and you'll walk down other piers but you have to remember: you do not need to board this boat."*
*– 6 Balloons, Marja-Lewis Ryan*

There's a finite amount of suffering, to take the thorn from one's hand is to put it in another. But do we thank those who seem to be lumbered with all the bad luck? No. We sympathise and say we're sorry only to thank God or the stars or the universe that it's not us. It's not us that has to be going through what they are. I'm not starving, I'm not dealing with death but I'm sorry for those who are and that's it. For someone to truly invalidate someone else's feelings because there are people who are truly suffering, that's what it's like to really not care.

People will analyse and pick at every word you've said but fail to realise that none of this is for you, you who reads this now, it's for myself. If you find solace in what I have to say that's nothing to do with me; I'm simply a catalyst to your own feelings.

Does that sound pretentious? Does that hit a nerve? Does that make you reach inside and wish you could articulate them yourself?

I don't know. I wasn't there to preach or give answers. I was merely there to board another boat. As I looked down at the strangers smiling, bearded face, that's exactly what I did; I boarded another boat. I used my drunken, shaky hands and pushed against his hard and muscular chest, removing him from my body. He laughed, grinning and playfully trying to place his hands back on my waist. His lips moved closer towards mine and I turned my head. Pulling my jacket back over my shoulders and my jeans back up my waist.

"Thanks!" I slurred, moving from the cubicle and letting the music from the dance floor flow through my body. I checked myself in the mirror, fixing the stray hairs and making brief eye contact with the stranger as he stood up from his kneeling position.

"You fucking tease!" he exclaimed, as I winked in response before turning and leaving the bathroom, immediately throwing myself onto the dancefloor. As I turned around to look at the door, I saw the man leave and head to the bar. Immediately surrounded by more sweating and writhing men, some shirtless, some wearing their confidence as their only outfit, I threw myself in the middle to be devoured. The strobe lights continued and as I rhythmically moved in time with the numerous bodies that surrounded me, every muscle that glistened with sweat I caught the eye of the bearded stranger. He pushed passed the others, still smiling before handing me another drink. Without hesitation, I finished the entire plastic cup. They teach us in school to never accept a drink we didn't make ourselves but that's another boundary that can easily be pushed so long as it's offered with a smile. The stranger leaned in close, so I could feel his warm breath on the nape of my neck before shouting through the music, "My name's Pete." I smiled again.

"Thanks!" I yelled back as his hands were on my waist.

"Is that the only word you know?" he laughed, moving our bodies close together.

"I didn't ask!" turning away from him so he stood behind me, our bodies moving in perfect synchronicity. For a moment as we felt the bass through the floor and each other. I turned back to face him as the lights continued to flash. I had no sense of time in this place, had I been drinking for hours or minutes? Had this flirtation gone back and forth the entire time? I reached into my jacket and pulled the cigarettes from the packet, placing one between my teeth and one in his mouth, using one finger to pull at his tank top I moved for the door. As we stepped on to the street, I reached for my phone. Remembering where I left it I whispered, "Shit!" as the stranger lit my cigarette for me, then his.

"So, you do know other words!" he joked.

"I know quite a few actually. It's Chris by the way," I lied, attempting to make conversation.

"Ah, smart and cute. Aren't I the lucky one?" he continued to flirt. In my experience, strange men that feed your addiction, whether they know about it or not, only want one thing and it was never a polite chat.

"Indeed. Listen, you seem really great and clearly you're very confident but your judge of character is absolutely shocking." I took a drag from the cigarette as we could still hear the music from the club. "You saw me at the bar and thought that I was cute so you bought me a drink in order to get a way in but let me tell you something; I'm an awful person!" I sarcastically remarked, smiling and throwing my cigarette to the ground. "It was nice to meet, Pete." I waved before stumbling passed him, grazing his shoulder.

"That's not true, I mean you're a bit selfish sure," he lightly grabbed my arm forcing me to face him.

"Exactly. I imagine most of the strangers you blow in cubicles are," I grinned, gently slipping my arm away. I began to walk down the street.

"Ouch, the puppy has a bite!" he remarked, throwing his cigarette to the floor as he began to follow.

"Woof!" I remarked back, as he joined my side. I could feel the euphoria as it continued to course through my body, the drugs and alcohol made the world disappear. "Okay, if you're going to insist on getting to know me, or stalk me, whatever this is, the least you could do is order an uber." I began flirting again. I remembered the cash in my wallet and how heavy it felt, yet I would let Pete foot the bill, mostly because I'd left my phone on the floor but also because a man should know nothing was for free.

"You're a cheeky little puppy, aren't you?" he pulled his phone from his pocket, opening the app to our location, passing it to me for the address. "Whilst your there, you can add your number," he said as I began to type the address. I hit request and watched as the icon was less than two minutes away.

"I don't have a phone," I replied, handing him back his. I turned my pockets out, holding onto my keys and my wallet as a car pulled up.

"What so I pay for your uber, your drinks and you just go on home?" He stood in the street with his phone in hand, like a rejected school boy. As I reached for the car door, I turned my head to smile.

"Who said it was just me going home?" I winked. Holding the door open as he climbed inside. I followed.

The ride was quiet as he tried to ask probing questions. The uber pulled up outside of my building. We thanked the driver as I could see the shop beneath the flat that was still open. I headed for the door as Pete followed behind. The shop assistant smiled at my familiar face.

"Grab a mixer…Litre Smirnoff please?" I asked, pulling a twenty-pound note from the wad of cash that was nestled so neatly inside my wallet. Pete placed two bottles of coke beside the litre. The shop assistant nodded and began typing the totals in to the till. "Anything else Pete?" He simply shook his head. "Pack of twenty of the usual as well please, also Pete look in that corner." I pointed my finger towards the security camera as the clerk added a pack of cigarettes to my total, making me remove another ten.

126

"What was that?" He laughed as I settled my bill, placing the cigarettes in my jacket and taking the vodka from the counter.

"So I know I won't get Jeffery Dhamere'd. Can never be too careful with who you bring into your home sweet pea," I said dryly. I heard the clerk chuckle as we left the shop and went up to the flat. The key turned and the door was opened allowing us to enter the dark and empty flat. He followed closely behind me and shut the door as I moved into the living room. As I placed the bottle on the table, I hadn't noticed a slip of paper that was left on the edge. Pete placed his bottles next to mine. "Glasses are through there, top cupboard," I said, unscrewing the lid of the vodka and pointing toward the kitchen. I started drinking straight from the bottle before he returned with two tall half-pint glasses, I had stolen from a local pub. He placed them on the table.

"So, do you live here alone?"

"Apparently so," I replied, pouring more than double measures we would have received if we had stayed in that night club. He dropped the small, plastic bag next to our drinks.

"Cool speakers, do you mind?" he asked and before I could answer, he had turned them on and plugged in his phone. I opened the bag and made two, clean lines like the ones we had done before. I had decided to not look at the time, for me this was a place that time couldn't touch. I had made the choice to find a simple touch wherever I could and to see that laid out against a canvas of everything I had built was a step in a direction I had never considered. We both crouched over the table, with one rolled note between us, taking it in turns, sniffing the lines up and letting the burning sensation hit the back of my throat. The music continued to play and as the high hit us I began to lose control once more. In this space, there was no today or tomorrow, no yesterday or even a past to think about because in this moment, that's where I was living.

# Chapter 15
## *Track 15 – Patty Griffin*
## *– Nobody's Crying*

As I sat on the end of my bed, my TV was stuck between channels, showing nothing but a blue screen. Pete was lying beside me, silent and still. His naked body was half-covered by the sheets that we had earlier been entangled in. The blue light filled the room. I saw nothing, no past or present and as I stared at Pete's perfectly trimmed beard, he slowly became Chris.

It was a few years ago, Chris had laid in bed for a few hours before I could wake him and as I stared in his direction, he began to open his eyes slowly. I smiled. He was partially covered by a thin sheet, laying on his front, his biceps rippling beneath his pillow. The sun had begun to pour in to our hotel room, we were in Rome. It was our first trip together. As he slowly opened his eyes, he smiled, looking me in the eye before turning over. I laughed before throwing my own naked body on to his.

"Come on, we'll miss the crowds for the colosseum if we leave soon," I said, poking and prodding making him squirm in bed. The day seemed so clear and remained vivid in my mind.

"Hey!" Pete's voice called out. I was back in my room, bathed in the blue light of the TV screen. I focused on his face, before turning my head towards the dresser opposite the bed. Two lines of white were laid out. "It seemed like you were somewhere else for a second," he spoke with sincerity, a sincerity that could only have come from a lie. As I stood up from the bed, I realised I was naked and feebly attempted to preserve my modesty before moving towards the dresser.

"For a moment, I was," I said, cryptically, keeping the blanket wrapped around my body. I grabbed the note that remained beside and took one line up, followed by the next. "You're probably going to want to leave soon," I said, looking him in the eye. He smiled, laughed slightly, before joining me by the table. His arm slowly moved up mine and he leaned in and kissed my neck, grinning with every move. I was high, I was still drunk and if I was being honest, I couldn't remember the last few hours that had led us to this point.

"What makes you say that puppy?" he quipped.

"Don't call me that!" I remarked back, pushing on his chest, keeping the sheets against my body. I moved back towards the bed. I looked him in the eye one last time before moving my naked body toward the bathroom. As I had done so many times before, I turned the tap and let the water run. The tiles were cold on my feet. I closed my eyes and when I did, I saw the night before in flashes of blue and green. The sweat between mine and a strangers naked body, the drinks and drugs that I so effortlessly inhaled even flashes of Pete and I moving into one another. I opened my eyes and noticed Pete's hand on my shoulder. I dropped the blanket and let his naked body lean into mine as he kissed my neck once again.

"Is this a metaphor for needing to be clean," he whispered, jokingly and as I cringed slightly, I brushed him off.

"Not everything is a fucking metaphor, sometimes things just are the way they are," I replied, leaning over to turn the water off.

"Everything can be, if you look hard enough," he said as I turned and laughed. I sat down on the edge of the bath, he knelt before me, taking me in his mouth once more. The alcohol and cocaine still coursed through both of our bodies. We repeated the same dance we had done before and as I tilted my head back allowing the blood to rush to all the parts of my body that mattered, he ran his hand up my body and onto my chest, lightly grabbing my throat. I lifted one hand from the bathtub side to place it on his head as I groaned. I lost my balance and fell backwards. Landing in the water and soaking the both of us. We both laughed and I remained in the water.

"What was that a metaphor huh?" I giggled. Time still hadn't found us. I stared into his hungry eyes, propping myself in the shallow water. "Now, be a dear and grab me a cigarette," I ordered, moving my entire body into the bath, sitting up right in the water.

"You tease!" he repeated, as he left the room briefly returning with two, one in his mouth and the other extended to me, shortly followed by a lighter. He had lit both cigarettes and as I inhaled, he shut the door behind him, stepping into the water opposite me. Our feet were sat on either side of each other as I flicked ash directly into the water.

"So, what's your thing then? Like what's your deal, some young, fit guy has a killer flat in the middle of the city alone? I don't buy it!" Pete began, inhaling his cigarette as we spoke.

"My thing is clearly meeting rugged strangers in bars and forgetting I exist, like every millennial," I joked, splashing him gently. I watched with intent as the droplets slowly rolled from his bulky chest and down through his chiselled stomach. I smiled as my eyes trailed further below and to what was floating beneath the surface.

"I'm being serious, you've never found anyone, never loved anyone enough to share this with?" he splashed back.

"We never love anyone. Not really. We only love our idea of another person. It's some concept of our own that we love, we love ourselves in fact," I remarked, finishing my cigarette and flicking it into the toilet bowl. "William Boyd, Any Human Heart!" I quoted. "Besides, sharing everything with someone is overrated, we've spent less than twenty-four hours with each other and you want to ask me about love and what I want to share with people? Where's your damage? What's your thing?" I asked. He finished his cigarette and placed it in the toilet. "I mean a ripped, totally masc-for-masc gay guy that gets by on cringey cliché's and goes home with young fit guys on a weekday also seems hard to believe," I finished.

"Cute and intelligent, I see. Literature your thing then? Or is it just deflecting?" he observed. He grinned at me and as hard as I tried, I could barely be offended by the truth.

"Why can't it be both? Or perhaps I'm just a mystery you'll never figure out, stick that up your metaphor and smoke it," I jibed, still deflecting, obviously. We both laughed. "What are you, a psychologist?" I said as we stopped laughing and one of his hands found its way on to my shin. I looked him straight in the eye. He smiled, taking a short breath, naked and sincere he sat before me in the water. Maybe everything was a metaphor if I did look hard enough, maybe this stranger that sat in the water before me, naked, was a metaphor for everyone I needed to open up to? Afterall, we were both strangers sharing an intimate moment and perhaps this one person asking me to share who I was my way out. He continued to smile as he spoke.

"I'm not. But I like to read people. You've been the most interesting so far. You went out of your way to make sure people knew I was here and then decided I needed to leave after staring into a blank television for. God knows how long, you invited me back after pushing me away and after dancing with me and let me touch you," he said, running his hand along the hairs on my leg. "Then when we get here alone, we do the drugs and keep drinking until the early hours and end up in this bath together; you're the king of mixed signals," he said as I retracted my leg from his grasp.

"Prince!" I replied, still keeping eye contact. His smile had stopped but hadn't turned malicious he had simply stopped. He knew what I meant and without missing a beat he started to speak.

"I'm not delusional, I know this won't go anywhere. I'm having fun, Chris."

The name shook me. I had forgotten that I had lied previously and I was reminded of the day before. In my mind, it flashed back to me laying before the door, unable to speak or move other than to reach for the alcohol I had stashed away. Everything that had lead me to this moment. "Good. Me too." I stood up from the shallow bath and removed myself from the bathroom and into the bedroom. "I'm glad we're on the same page," I called back as I walked, wet and naked to the bedroom. I heard the splashing of the water as he hastily followed behind me. As I entered the room, I began to grab at the clothes that were strewn across the floor. I noticed vodka left in the bottle and reached for that, taking a sip. Pete shortly followed catching me mid-sip.

"You want to know me? You want to know why I don't share all of me? This, this is it!" I shouted, holding the bottle at arm's length. "Sometimes we share ourselves entirely with someone and sometimes who we share isn't pretty, or nice or someone that anyone would fall in love with or want to be loved by." I continued, throwing the clothes I had gathered to the bed. We both remained naked, dripping on the carpet. "People always ask you to be yourself but the minute you are unapologetically yourself or show some side that's not desirable you're written off as some hopeless case!" I shouted, pacing around the room. Perhaps it was the cocaine, perhaps it was the alcohol but it just kept coming. I moved to the bag again, pouring two more lines and as I racked them up, I noticed Pete's face. He stood in the doorway completely naked and blank.

"You could never love anyone because you don't love yourself and maybe I don't know you because I don't myself, you don't even know you. Who are you?" he asked, softly and sincerely. He began to move towards me, I had already grabbed the rolled-up note that remained on the table, he took it from my hands. We shared a moment, brief and intimate, but as he took the note from my hand, I could see what he wanted. We were both as high as each other and as drunk as each other. He leant over and sniffed up a completely clean line, handing me the note after. I took the line up without a thought.

"I am me. I'm an asshole. An alcoholic and a cheat. I never do anything by half and I apparently don't give a damn for other people's feelings and you're right. Maybe I can't love anyone or even think about it," I began to stumble, I was suddenly notified of my nakedness. I scrambled for some coverage, a pair of underwear just slipping over my slightly damp body. "What do you want from me?" I dejectedly asked, not expecting a sensible answer.

"Who is James?" he asked. He almost whispered the question and I responded with a blank expression. I was reminded that I had given a false name and immediately became defensive.

"What the fuck are you talking about?" I asked, keeping everything I had close to my chest.

"There's a letter downstairs for James, I glanced over it when I attempted to clean up last night," he replied, innocently and still naked. I moved passed him in the doorway, heading for the stairs. As I entered the living room, the slip of paper that had once sat underneath the bottle of vodka. As I picked it up and pulled it close to my face, I began to cry. I read the words that were hand written by him:

*"I'm sorry about what has happened over the past month but I know it's for the best. For both of us. I'm going to miss you a lot. Please don't be afraid to contact anyone if you need help. Stay strong."*

He had signed it in his endearing, childlike handwriting and the tears kept flowing.

# Chapter 16
## *Track 16 – Kat Cunning*
## *– King of Shadow*

Have you ever been lost? At some point in your journey you took a wrong turn or were misdirected and now you have no idea where you are so you frantically look for signs or strangers that would be willing to send you the right way and get you to your destination. If you were lucky, you weren't lost for very long and you got home safe eventually and the whole experience was just a funny story you told to everyone you met that day.

Have you ever felt lost even though you know exactly where you're going? You're walking along the street and you've mapped out every turn, all the best traffic lights to cross at because they change the second you press the button and you know all the best times of day to take each street depending on how many people you can deal with yet somehow, you still have no idea where you're going? It's that same frantic panicked feeling deep in your chest accompanied by numbness in your head. Being lost within yourself can sometimes feel worse however because there isn't a right or wrong answer.

The saying goes that when God closes a door, he opens a window. However, this house is on fire and the windows are locked and it's located in the middle of a dark forest that's going to burn down just as easily. I've said previously that nobody's watching you so you may as well just do what you want but that's not entirely true. People do watch to an extent and their houses will burn down with yours, if you let them.

However, nobody said God kept the door locked. Sometimes there is only one way, only one path forward and to do that, you have to keep the door open. Nobody wants to crawl through the window like a kidnap victim or burglar of your own life, it's simply not helpful.

I've found honesty is like opening a door you can't lock up again. The most effective key. Once you've told the truth, once you've realised your own truth and opened that door to everyone around you it's impossible to lock it back up. The truth may not necessarily always stay as the truth it can change as can secrets. For example, hundreds of years ago, it was true that the world was flat and before that it was true that extinction was a myth because God wouldn't destroy his own creations. So, with that in mind it may be true that I'm suffering from depression and other mental health issues. It's true that I have a severe drinking problem. But that doesn't mean it'll always be true.

Owning up to when you've done wrong or simply allowing people to know the truth can keep that door open and let everyone around you help put out that fire. Own the house you live in.

There's a point when you look in the mirror and the words fall from your mouth "who the fuck are you?" I was doing that, with the letter in my hand as I began to shake. Now correct me if I'm wrong, identity crises are far and few between but when you look at yourself day after day and all that you can quote is Meredith Brooke's 'Bitch' something needs to change.

I can't speak for everyone but I can speak for myself. I know that over the years, I had given as good as I got, I'd fought my corner even though I wasn't necessarily winning. It's that nature that had gotten me through. It was not healthy, however, to run from everything. That was something I'd mastered, the mentality that if I couldn't see it then it couldn't see me but the truth is it was still there. It always will be, the feeling of not being good enough or the feeling of embarrassment will linger. It's something that I have come to terms with and given myself to. All this time I've had it in me but sometimes I needed a push. Pete's observation of my character had given me this.

I think that eventually everyone's luck runs out and once it does it's the wakeup call you need. Most of us avoid having to get there but for those of us that have to reach that point before we finally stop and think of my initial question, it's needed. People look towards you as some kind of confident people person but it's all a game, it's something I've learnt to master. I had constantly won, I was able to fool everyone into believing me and I was able to function as 'normal' without a single person batting an eyelid.

As of late, I had a self-destruct button pushed well and truly in. It was over. I was done playing the victim and I would not continue this way. I would resume life as normal. I decided to work and continue to pick fights and answer rhetorics with sarcasm and chose to love the way I did.

As Pete descended from the stairs, I wiped the tears from my face and he continued on.

"You need to leave, now." I said, as I pushed him aside and moved upstairs to change my clothes. He looked at me with a sense of disappointment. He followed closely behind.

"Really? You're just gonna make me leave?" he asked, standing in the doorway of my bedroom. I grabbed at the clothes I had worn the night before and included the denim jacket.

"I don't care where you go, I'm leaving. I'm gone!" I responded, moving towards the stairs. He tried to grab me and I shook him off. As I entered the living room, I could see my bag and before I could grab at what was inside, Pete's voice called from above.

"Where are you going?!" he screamed. I placed the bag over my shoulder.

"Home, you should too sweet pea!" I called back, leaving the flat and entering on to the street.

I moved to the platform, slowly and stumbling taking it one step at a time. My bag weighed heavier than I'd expected, perhaps it was the money or maybe it was the bottle that continuously knocked against my legs. I stood waiting for the

CPSIA information can be obtained
at www.ICGtesting.com
Printed in the USA
LVHW050742270420
654450LV00011B/1080

train, with tears in my eyes, looking towards all the people on the other side. Did they know? Did they see me? I looked at the schedule above my head; 3 minutes. As I turned my head to look towards the stairs that lead from the station to the various platforms available, I could see various feet, various pairs of shoes mixing and belonging to the various different people that would need to get a train that day. I saw his shoes slowly descend the station. With each step, I looked on with hope, hope was medicine for the soul and I was sick and tired.

I saw Chris' face, his eyes were as kind and gentle as they had always been as he ran into my arms. We cried and he begged me not to leave as I fell into his warm and comforting embrace. His rough, large hands wiped the tears from my face and we kissed, it felt more important than any kiss we had shared before. As I felt his lips on mine, a train passed by snapping me out of the reverie I had put myself in.

I stood on the platform alone. Chris wasn't there and as the train began to slow down, I started to think of every moment that had passed by, every second that had lead up to this point. The strangers looked on opposite and ignored the tears as they continued to roll down my cheeks. I was sent back to thinking about the blue ghost, how easy it would have been to take a few more steps and how none of this would've happened if I had followed. Chris wasn't going to descend from the station and he wasn't going to be my shoulder to cry on anymore—the train stopped. As the doors opened, I looked towards the stairs one last time, hoping, praying to see those shoes one last time. Anything to stop me from leaving but I knew what was right and what was wrong. That's what the money was for, it wasn't to stay silent or to forget, it was to leave, start over. The doors opened. I boarded the train.